TulipTree
review

SPRING/SUMMER 2024
issue #15

Wild Women

TULIPTREE
PUBLISHING, LLC

Contents

Our Fairy Tale

Victoria Castañeda

Winter's wind coldly whispered into my uncovered ears, while the Rio Grande below me was lifelessly silent. I looked around and as far as I could see in both directions was the red-brown border wall blazing through the desert, a monstrous monument to America's desire to control the uncontrollable. I was coming to the end of the pedestrian bridge that connects downtown El Paso to Juarez, leading straight onto the bar-filled strip that even at noon was booming with reggaeton. Hunched against February's cold and my own fear, I ignored the calls of "taxi, taxi!" from groups of men waiting on each side of the street. After a couple of blocks, I saw a deserted restaurant and quickly went inside, sat at a table, and ordered a bottle of water. I wanted to call an Uber to the airport away from unwanted stares: I rarely took taxis off the street in Mexico City, and I was surely not going to do it in Juarez, a city famous for the mutilated bodies of kidnapped girls.

I made the decision long before my trip to the border that I wasn't going to contact my father, but holding my phone in my hand, when my thumb hit request, the finality erased any lingering uncertainty. The uncertainty had been new, barely appearing a few months before when I was in Alabama visiting family. After a nephew's little league soccer game, a few of us had gone to eat lunch, where I'd mentioned to my aunt Micaela that I had an upcoming work trip to Juarez and El Paso, the place where my family is from. She immediately and unexpectedly began imploring me to contact my father. I stared blankly into my cup of coffee as she told me how she'd seen him on her last trip to Juarez: "I ran into him at his butcher shop. When he saw me, he asked about you, not even whispering, 'Y Victoria?' In front of his employees and everything."

"What did you tell him?" I asked, holding back a smile at the absurdity of "running into" someone at their workplace. I was curious to see what she'd shared, as she had a habit of incorrectly informing everyone that I was a business graduate from Harvard (I don't know if she actually thinks that's true or just true enough, but I leave her to it).

"You know. I told him you went to Harvard. That you even got a master's and how proud we were. You should reach out to him, mami. It might give you some answers." The pride she felt that he hadn't whispered my name gave me answers enough, but I said I'd think about it. I didn't mean it when I said it, but then I did start to think about it, sheepishly asking my mother if she thought it might be worth it. She was kindly diplomatic. "That's up to you, but I don't see what you'd get out of it."

Arriving at the airport in Juarez three hours early, I sat on a leather couch in the lounge overlooking the ramp, pulled out a novel, and ordered glass after glass of wine. *Well, that's that*, I thought. My indifference felt intoxicating.

I met my father once, when I was seven years old, crossing that same bridge from El Paso to Juarez and back. I have no recollection of his face or his voice or anything about him really. Rather, I remember objects and my emotional responses to them. A rusty hand saw in the back seat of his car cutting my thumb and my shame for being so careless as I wordlessly wiped my blood on the bottom of the seat. A small white ceramic bowl of arroz con leche sprinkled with raisins and cinnamon and my exuberance at the luxury of ordering dessert. A gray industrial metal shelf running the length of a sterile bookstore where I was told to pick any book I wanted and my slight indignation at such a small gift.

My only clear memory of that day is walking back to El Paso with my mother, squeezed between the metal railings on the narrow concrete bridge. Under the afternoon's sun, I watched the sweat-marked back of the *fronterizo* in front of me. Everyone had papers in hand, all of us hoping to quickly enter and leave the squat glass and metal building that controlled the entrance to America.

My mother and I were unlucky. After showing our papers, I was taken aside into a tiny room with glass walls and seated in a black plastic chair. My short legs swinging, I gave the story I had been asked to memorize, its three simple parts: we were visiting my father in Juarez, my mother lived in Alabama, and the woman I was with was Norma, a family friend from Texas.

After being told to wait, my thighs became slick with sweat springing up like dew. Placed carefully on my lap was the book my father had bought me, *My Favorite Fairy Tales*. I stared at its turquoise cover, memorizing every detail of the illustration: a blonde, long-haired princess crouching down by a pond, her sparkling white dress spread around her as she reaches toward a floating frog prince. I observed the princess to ignore that I was being observed by the female US Border Patrol agent in green uniform standing in the corner with her arms crossed.

The wooden door opened and a man in the same uniform came in who, like me and like her, had brown skin and dark hair. He leaned in, hands on his belt, to whisper to her in Spanish, "They're giving the same story. And the girl's birth certificate does say Birmingham."

I looked out the window so they wouldn't see understanding in my eyes. I felt them both turn to look at me. The woman responded in a Spanish marred by assimilation, "But they look so alike. There's no way they're not related."

Then they said it was time to go, and I slid off the chair, holding the book firmly to my chest, and followed them down a hallway lined with more black plastic chairs. My mother was sitting there, waiting. I knew not to call her mami but smiled to let her know I had done a good job: we were allowed to leave. She grabbed my sweaty hand, and we walked out into the sunlight, descending the bridge into downtown El Paso to catch a bus to my grandmother's in San Elizario. Once there, I grabbed a blue pen tightly in my hand, confident I knew my letters for such a simple phrase: "My dad gave me this book on March 26, 2002."

By 2002, the border was no longer the place my mother had grown up in. Before 9/11, the border belonged to the fronterizos who lived there, crossing back and forth as they wished, uninterested in laws or the nations that made them. Before 9/11, if you didn't have papers, you could swim across the river or pay a man five pesos to drag you across on a tire. For those who spoke English, like my mother, you could simply lie and say "American" at the checkpoint. If you were caught at one bridge, you tried another. After 9/11, Uncle Sam's fear fell heavily over the border, and fronterizos' lives became defined by control rather than fluidity.

March 26, 2002, was one of the few times I played a role in rolling the dice alongside my undocumented mother, silently hoping luck was on our side. Like every other close call, it was never discussed. Talking about fear was forbidden in our household, even though it prowled on the edges of our lives, occasionally baring its fangs in moments like these. With silence, we kept fear at bay and didn't waste energy worrying about potential misfortune. Silence was also my mother's approach to my father. I knew that I'd inherited my love of reading from him, along with my thick hair and fat toes. At some point as a teenager, I also learned that he was married and had two daughters older than me. Beyond these facts, I didn't know much else and didn't ask, respecting my mother's rule of silence.

I started interviewing my mother a few weeks after my trip to Juarez, as I sat in a wooden rocking chair by my balcony and she sat comfortably on my bed surrounded by pillows. I was living in Mexico City working with nonprofits in migrant rights, and she had come to visit me. It was early April, and Mexico City's jacarandas were in full bloom outside my window. Somewhere on the street outside, a man played the tune to *"Bésame mucho"* on a saxophone. As I got ready to begin the interview, the shield of apathy I had been hiding behind began to crumble. My mother had agreed to be interviewed, to share her life with me without qualms. Able to ask her anything, my father and the day I met him was the first thing I wanted to know about. After a lifetime of waiting, I was hoping against all logic to hear that my father was special and that I was special to him. I began with a simple question to hide my desperation: "What do you remember about the day I met my dad?"

After a pause, she said, "I don't remember that day, mami." I looked at her while trying to hide my disbelief. She lifted her eyebrows and scrunched her mouth slightly to one side in a slightly apologetic expression. I recited all the disconnected details from my memory believing they would spark something. Nothing.

"How could you forget? We even got stopped," I said.

"I don't know. I guess it wasn't that important to me," she admitted. I kept insisting. She became exasperated. There was nothing I could do to fight her disremembrance as it seized my childish hope from me and threw it into a river of insignificance, so I breathed and allowed the remnants of any possible idealization of my father to float away from me before I moved on with the interview: "Well . . . then . . . How did you meet my dad?"

Asking about a father long lost is a wonderful path toward finding yourself in awe at the strength a mother found.

My mother met Martin when she was working as a *cantinera* near the strip in Juarez. She was twenty years old and was raising my two-year-old brother alone. *"I worked in the maquilas, first, but it was very little pay. Things were going really well for me being a cantinera. I'm not even gonna say a bartender, since I never made drinks. I would dress pretty and talk to the customers. Flor, an older cantinera, told us how to behave—'Look, talk to the customers, make them feel good, because they're going to leave you a tip.' When customers went to the cantina, your job was to entertain them."*

My mother has photos from the cantinas taken by photographers who charged 10 pesos. When I'd seen them as a child, I'd imagined they were memories from a night out with friends. In all of them, young women with dramatic makeup sporting homemade dresses smile broadly as they sit atop bar stools and pool tables. In those photos, my mother has coffee-colored eyebrows and wine-red lipstick. That and her hair, the way her bangs are puffed out on top, reveal the photos to be from the nineties. Other than that, she looks the same as when I was growing up: joyful and bold, wearing clothes that show off her slender legs, tiny waist, and large chest.

"I didn't know that it was narcos in the cantinas at first. I learned it working there and realized, 'Oh!' I told my sister, 'Marcela, come on. Come work here, you'll do really well, too.' She already had Miguel, but our mom was worried because she thought that Marcela was too pendeja." Marcela was also a single mother, eighteen with a four-year-old, yet the idea of working in the cantinas surrounded by narcos scared her, as it would most young women. My mother, on the other hand, has always used bravery bordering on recklessness as her main tool in her search for a better life.

The women my mother met in the cantinas were similar to my family in that they or their mothers had migrated from rural parts of Mexico to work in the maquilas, or factories, that line the border. In contrast to small towns, in the maquilas, it didn't matter if you were a virgin, if you went to church, if you had a bastard child, or if you were a bastard child. It just mattered that your work was cheaper than a man's. Mexico's industrialization at the border almost seemed to propel a feminist movement, until these women realized that the pay wasn't enough. For those brave enough to work at night in a city where girls were disappearing in the darkness, tapping into the growing narco economy as cantineras became a better option.

"JB was where all of the narcos would get together. That's why everybody liked to work there. It was the same owner as the first cantina I worked in, Erika's. I really wanted to go to JB because that's where the money was. Narcos were loose with their money, and I just wanted whoever was most generous. Almost all of them were married, and married men are a bit easier to control because they really don't want a relationship with you. The ones chasing after me were always married, and since I was only going out with them because they were loose with their money, if they left me a good tip, I'd say, 'Okay you're worthy of my time.' I just saw dollar signs, especially if they came from the US. All of the girls there, we would talk amongst ourselves, "Oh this güey has dollars.' So we knew who had dollars. They left better tips. Sometimes they'd even leave a hundred-dollar bill.

"There was a woman who worked there that we all called her Pichitos, because she was good at saying, 'Me pichas?' Will you buy me this? She was always saying it, 'Me pichas? Me pichas?' For whatever, vendors coming in to sell roses or stuffed animals. Which I thought was tacky. 'Me pichas a rose?' A man should buy you a rose if he wants to. But seeing that she was never ashamed to do that, I started to learn a little bit. I learned to be more bold from seeing her, that she never got discouraged, and the customers rarely told her no. I didn't like to say, 'me pichas?' I thought that was too . . . I don't know, like a beggar. But it was normal, it was part of the culture, that if you were with a man, if you said, 'Oh, look at this!' to something, they would say, 'You want it?' So I would just say it like that, 'Oh, I like this.' 'You want it?' 'Sí.' I never . . . I was never with someone. No one was ever my boyfriend. I didn't have to be living with some man to get money out of them. I could get money out of men without living with them.

"That year, I bought your brother Javier lots of things from the Little Tykes brand. I bought him a slide from Little Tykes that had its stairs. Then I bought him a bench like a picnic table also from Little Tykes, and a little motorcycle that he could ride around. I bought him all that and a few other little things. I wanted to give your brother gifts. He *was my only son, and I had money to buy him those things. Miguel was older than your brother, three years older. Marcela got really bothered with me for buying him all those things, when she didn't have money to buy Miguel anything, and he was going to see that Santa Claus brought Javier these things. I told her, 'Come work in the cantinas, you make good money.' I had been telling her for a while, 'Marce, come work over here.' She didn't want to, didn't want to. Finally, I convinced her. Well . . . she already had Hugo, too. She didn't have a choice."*

All of the cantineras were young women navigating a landscape of misogyny and poverty to provide for their families, and it was in this environment that my mother met my father. While my hope for a fairytale story about him was burned to the ground, I couldn't help but to stand in the light of those flames and admire my mother.

My mother usually dated *panzones* because they had the most money. Martin and his seven brothers, los hermanos Ibarra, were regulars at JB, and all of them were panzones with an air of importance. The owner of the cantinas, an accountant who held meetings in his office where relinquishing your gun at the door was required, would make a point to come down and greet los hermanos whenever they came in.

"They had family businesses. I don't know if they had family businesses together or if each of them had a business. Maybe their parents had money, because they even went to study in Europe and the US. I don't know exactly where their money came from, but I never heard from the other girls that your dad and his brothers were narcos. He and all his brothers were great at dancing, and all the cantineras wanted to dance with them, los Ibarra. Martin was very polite, and I liked him for that. He didn't speak by yelling, like the narcos would, and he would use big words that I didn't know.

"I didn't know this about myself until recently, but I like to learn. And so that really caught my attention, the way he would talk about things. I would listen to him, thinking, 'Oh wow!' You know, some men like to talk, talk, talk, to try to impress you. Maybe your dad thought, 'Oh

look, I can impress this one,' and that's why he liked talking to me. I don't know, but I caught your dad's attention, and he started pursuing me very seriously. He never told me that he was married. Later I found out. One of the girls told me that all los hermanos Ibarra were married.

"That was very common, that you're going out with some güey, and that he's taking you around, 'Ay, my baby' and all that shit. That's common in Mexico, that men have their girlfriend and they treat her like a princess, taking you all over and buying you things and in their car. Like your dad. I'd be in his car, right next to him. All of this space, and he and I, right next to each other. And there were some men, even if they were married, that were really possessive. But at that point, I was going out with various men. I didn't care, I didn't take anyone seriously. Nobody. Because you'd be dating someone and then you'd find out they were married."

During the time she was dating Martin, things were going smoothly for my mother. A man who saw that most of the cantineras were her friends and that they had good chemistry working together offered her a job as manager at his new bar if she brought her friends with her. She took that job, and Martin, a longtime regular at JB, started going there instead. As manager, she made such good money that she bought her first car, a 1986 gold Ford Tiempo. Then one day, she started having stomach pains. "One of the cantineras told me, 'Go get checked, maybe you have cysts. I've had cysts before, and they're really painful.' I went to do a sonogram, and the doctor told me, 'There's your cyst.' There you were, moving around. I cried. And not from excitement. Or happiness. Your brother was older by then, he didn't need to be breastfed or a bottle. I was feeling comfortable. Then I found out I was pregnant with you."

Hearing this, I asked her, "Why did you decide to keep me?" I was still innocently searching for some evidence of a fairy tale in the ashes that lay at my feet. My mother looked at me carefully before responding, "No, mami. Didn't I tell you before? That I took a shot of tequila with pepper?"

"I don't think so. Tell me again."

"One of the cantineras told me that if I took a shot of tequila with a spoon of pepper, that supposedly the baby would come out. I did that. I thought I would fall to the floor in that instant in pain." She paused again before adding in a teasing tone, *"It didn't work, mami."*

The stability my mother felt she'd achieved shattered like glass after she became pregnant with me. She had to quit working, and one day she came home to find that her sister Micaela had totaled her car. My grandmother, a notorious yay-sayer even to the worst of ideas, had been the one to give her the keys. "Didn't you have insurance?" I asked, my innocence emerging again.

"Nada. I didn't even know what that was. I was super, super mad at my mom, enojadísima. *Like the Hulk. Or worse. And she kicked me out. I couldn't go with your dad, he was married, so I told him, 'Give me some money to go to Alabama. I'll have the baby there. My sister is there.'"* The sister in Alabama was Marcela, who had recently left Juarez and the cantinas to clean houses in Alabama, invited by a family friend. More than seven months pregnant, my mother flew to Birmingham with three-year-old Javier.

By the time my mother arrived in Alabama, Marcela wasn't able to live with the friend anymore, so she moved in with a man she was dating, along with Miguel and Hugo. The man was from Zacatecas, and in the trailer lived two other men from his town, all of them working in construction. My mother felt uncomfortable staying there, and she asked a cousin who lived in Alabama if she could stay with them until she gave birth. They said yes, and she moved in, although it was already six people. Her cousin, his wife and child, his wife's brother, his wife, and their children.

"When I moved in there, I don't know if someone snitched or not, but they told me it was too many people. So then Mike told me I had to go, me, the one there alone. They kicked me out because I wasn't contributing anything. Rosalba's sister's husband, he was working with

Mike, so he was contributing. I wasn't there like an arrimada. I would clean, make food, make tortillas for burritos or whatever. I did something, but they still kicked me out, and I ended up at the Salvation Army."

In general, my mother detests lamenting any situation. She calls such behavior *haciéndose la victima*, making yourself a victim. Yet I thought that with so much time having passed since she lived in the Salvation Army eight months pregnant, she would finally feel safe enough to lament the situation. Instead, she started happily reminiscing about the food she ate there. *"We were staying in the family area and because I was pregnant, they would give us snacks often, and I liked that a lot, that they gave us snacks. They would give us Hills . . . I can't remember the name, but it's a sausage tied like a horseshoe. We really liked it, but it was too expensive, so we never bought it. But there, they gave it to us every day!"* Reliving her old delight, she gasped and raised her eyebrows. I laughed at how fondly she remembered the Salvation Army as she justified her glee, *"It was yummy!"*

She only became angry when she started recounting calling Martin to announce my birth. *"I told him I'd named you Victoria, and he asked me, 'Why did you name the baby Victoria?' I thought to myself, Why is he asking me why I named you Victoria? Then . . . I kept thinking, like this, why he was asking me . . ."* She paused to look up in thought, then she suddenly put on a look of rage that was common when I was a child but has become less so as she's gotten older: her brows furrowed, chin pulled back a bit, looking you up and down. She sucked her teeth, before continuing, *"He thought I named you Victoria because it was a victory for me to have a child of his. And I told him, 'Estás pendejo! You're an idiot.' Right away I started telling him, 'Who do you think you are? Haven't you looked at yourself in the mirror?' I remember I told him many things . . . offensive things. Because he came to me with that. I told him, 'What do you think? What do you think I want? That you get a divorce and I get the grand prize of marrying you? You're a pinche pendejo, a fucking asshole.' He asked me why I named you*

Victoria. I was so, so mad, that he thought I was declaring victory for having his child."

Shortly after my birth, Marcela got a phone call that left them both feeling hopeful. It was my grandmother, telling them, "I found a home for us in El Paso!" When my mother had left for Alabama a couple months before, she'd been living with my grandmother in an apartment in Juarez. With a home in El Paso, the boys could study in American schools, a priority for both my mother and Marcela. They just needed to wait until I was two weeks old to fly back.

I'd known that I was born in Alabama, but I'd also known that we didn't live there until I was four. These interviews answered many of the questions I had growing up, not only about my father but also about my being born in Alabama. Then, I started getting more stories about our past from my aunts. It seemed that with distance, the hardship they'd gone through was now nothing more than obstacles lining the path up the mountain they had climbed. From the heights they'd reached, those obstacles now seemed small and harmless.

In September of 2023, the year I completed interviews with my mother, I went to Alabama for the board meeting of an education nonprofit I work with. My mother had just moved to a city in the green mountains of northwest Spain, so I stayed with my aunt Marcela, who by that time was the director of community engagement at Alabama's Spanish-language radio station. We were in her charcoal-gray Mercedes SUV heading to meet my uncle for lunch downtown. When we drove past a yellow brick building, Marcela said, "You see that building? That used to be a strip club. Your mom and I worked there when she was super pregnant with you."

"Dancing?" I asked, shocked.

She sucked her teeth at my stupid question. "No, dummy. As a waitress. It used to be called Lynn's Golden Lady. The owner was a white lady, but she was with some Mexican guy from Coahuila. His name was Fernando. Since there weren't any places for *los piojos* to go out drinking yet, they started having events in the evening for them, before the poor girls started dancing." Piojos means lice and is a derogatory term for poor, uneducated people.

"El Sol wasn't open yet?" I asked. El Sol is the dance club that caused a separation between my Mexican girlfriends and me when I was a teenager. Their parents started letting them go dance there at thirteen, fourteen years old. El Sol was a slice of Mexico, a club where no one was carded and where it was considered perfectly normal for grown men to gawk at the blossoming bodies of young girls. I would beg my mother to let me go, but she was unmoved, always telling me I had no business hanging out with a bunch of piojos.

"No, this was years before El Sol," Marcela responded. "El Sol opened in 2001. We announced their twenty-year anniversary a couple years ago on the radio. When were you born? 1994? Back then, there weren't that many Mexicans here for them to have a club yet. And there weren't any women. To see a mexicana was rare. That's why they hired me and your mom here to serve the drinks, even though she had her huge belly. Like this." She held her hand out from her stomach to show me how pregnant my mother was when she waited tables at this strip club, one of the first efforts in Birmingham to capitalize on the growing Mexican population.

I've researched Mexican immigration for years, but it is always moments like these where I am most struck by the harsh realities of being a single, undocumented mother. The more I learn about my mother's past, the more I am overcome by amazement for her. She came from a place lower than I had been able to imagine, standing as I was, up above, protected by privilege and innocence.

Two weeks after I was born, we flew to El Paso, arriving on a dark December night. My mother didn't know what to expect of the duplex my grandmother had procured, but she didn't expect what she showed up to. It had two rooms with boarded-up windows and no running water or electricity. My grandmother used a flashlight to guide my mother in as she held me carefully in her arms. Shining the flashlight into the largest room, my mother saw there was no furniture, only a spread of blankets on the floor where my grandmother, the three boys, my mother, Marcela, my youngest aunt, and I would sleep that first night.

During the night, the desert cold creeped into the house's darkness. In her telling, my mother didn't say how she felt arriving to this house with a newborn baby, instead simply saying, *"So then I told your dad that I got back to my mom's and there's nothing. He gave me money right when I got there to get a toilet installed. Then we tried me living in Juarez with you and your brother. Your dad rented me a house, but that didn't work out too long."*

"Why didn't it work out?" I asked, knowing that her lack of diplomacy can be an asset or a defect depending on the situation.

"I was dating someone else, and your dad didn't like that. A guy called El Guey. I met him at one of the cantinas, too. I think he was a narco. He would take me out to eat Chinese food. Chinese food was really fancy for us, because it was different, and to eat out was something really fancy, to eat at a restaurant. El Guey knew I was with your dad, and he wanted me to be with him, so he made me a hickey by force. I told him no, and he made me a hickey against my will so that Martin would see it. Later I found out El Guey was married, too. He said he wasn't, until, one day I saw him with a woman. He did like this to me, look." She paused and turned her head to look at me from the corner of her eye, then shook her head imperceptibly. *"I told your dad, I'm not your wife, and I'm not your girlfriend. You're the father of my child. You're giving me child support to pay the rent. But he said, 'Why would I pay your rent if you're seeing other men,' and I don't know what else. It became a while thing, and you know how I am. Then, I went back to El Paso."*

Even across the border, the easiest place for her to find work was in a cantina. She started working as a waitress at Kumbala, a cantina used to launder money that was owned by a narco she had been seeing for years. One night at 2 a.m., Kumbala was shot up by a rival cartel, killing everyone inside except for the one man chosen as the messenger, who survived with a broken leg.

After a few months, my mother stopped working there, but not because it was filled with narcos. Rather, she couldn't bear the danger of relying on a single man for her livelihood, and she left to work at one of the few places she could get a job without papers, a strip club called Nero's.

On the first day of spring break my freshman year of college, I was sitting at the gate at SFO waiting to board my first flight on the way home to Birmingham. On my lap lay a book about the drug trade in Juarez. Since starting college, I had been checking out the books that appeared when I searched the city's name in the Stanford Libraries catalog, quickly learning that Juarez was a city dominated by violence due to drug cartels' constant struggle for control of its trafficking routes.

I had just finished a chapter explaining how cartels bring profits from sales in the US back to Mexico using "couriers." Incredulous, I called my mother to share what I was reading, telling her how one could make thousands of dollars for crossing the border with money hidden on their body or in their car. She didn't seem surprised when she said, "Sometimes they'll try to get a woman with children to go with them so they look like a family. It's less suspicious."

"How do you know that?"

"Oh, you know." My mother says this when she has a lot to say on something but doesn't want to say it. It's usually in a coy, slightly high-pitched tone. She always makes the same face when she says it, looking you right in the eyes, lifting her brows up slightly, and smiling wryly, lips pursed, "Oh, you know."

"You've never mentioned that to me," I said.

"There was no reason for you to know."

It was almost time to board, so I didn't push it. When it was my time to board, I hung up, then stood to wait in line, as I processed the realization that my mother had lived other lives before me, and that they were lives that marked her as a different person, a changed person. Growing up, she had been strict and demanding; it shocked me to think she could be involved with something like smuggling. Smuggling was a criminal activity. My mother wasn't a criminal.

The more I thought of it, however, smuggling was only black or white if you assessed it through a certain lens. Through the lens of legality, it was as black as the text that would be on your criminal record. Seen through the lens of caring for one's children, it was white, pure hope, a blank slate of opportunity being sought in the only way accessible.

I boarded my flight and took my seat. On the flight, my curiosity dispelled as I sank into lightness. I was getting to go home after finding my first months in college lonely.

Ten years after that flight, in the context of our interviews, I could now ask my mother to tell me more about what she meant that day on the phone. She began by making it clear that she *never* smuggled drugs: "*I may be a lot of things, but I'm not a pendeja. Well, I didn't bring it. Not knowingly.*" She then told me of when she started working at Nero's when I was almost a year old, shortly after my father stopped supporting us. At Nero's, she met a man named Mario, who drove a brand-new, silver Dodge Ram pickup truck, dressed well, and wore expensive cologne. He was an Indigenous man with jet-black hair and cinnamon-colored skin, from some part of southern Mexico she can't remember. "*He'd come visit me sometimes in Nero's, and he'd put a bunch of twenties in my g-string.*" She paused to lift her chin up slightly and added, "*Not that he was the only one who'd do that.*"

Mario would occasionally ask her to accompany him, to Juarez or New Mexico, to pick a car up or drop one off or to make a quick stop. All she had to do was sit there, maybe spend the night somewhere. I asked her innocently, "Why do you think he knew you'd be open to going with him?"

"*Because he offered me money, and I was a stripper. Strippers do things for money.*"

The first time she accompanied Mario, they drove to Juarez in his Dodge pickup truck. "*We parked in a body shop, and I thought, huh, something is gonna happen here. But nothing happened.*" He got out of the truck. She waited. He got back in the truck. "*All he had was a cup of McDonald's soda, with a straw in there and everything. He put it in the cup holder and that was it. Just a little cup.*" Then they drove back to El Paso, and he gave her money for her time. "*I remember that time so much, because I thought to myself, 'What did we come over here for?' But I would never ask him.*"

"*The second time, he said we were gonna go pick up a car from New Mexico someplace . . . Mami!*" she exclaimed. Our interviews are sprinkled with her cutting herself off to exclaim "Mami!" in excitement over some forgotten episode just resurfaced. "*Mami! You don't remember this probably, but remember this picture where you have worms on your back for fishing and we're next to a lake?*" I did; photos of me as a baby are scarce. In this photo, I'm in a diaper and lying on a blanket with my brother. My mother stands next to us, wearing a long, flowered brown dress and a button-down denim shirt tied in a knot. Her hair is dyed an unseemly shade of red, and one of her front teeth has a silver covering with a star carved into it. We look like nothing other than a happy family having a day by a lake. "*Mario told me he would take us to Elephant Butte. He had ulterior motives because what he really wanted was to take a family with him, but I wanted to take you guys. Basically I used someone else's means to be able to enjoy Elephant Butte. We even camped out there and made hamburgers. We were going with him to pick up a car in New Mexico.*"

"Was he nice to us?" I asked.

"*Yeah, he was nice to you guys. Well, that was the only time you actually met him.*" The day after the lake, we went to a car shop to pick up a car using a dolly, but when we arrived, Mario told my mother the car wasn't ready. Then he unhooked the dolly and started the two-hour drive back to El Paso. No car, no dolly . . . no questions. *"He never ever told me, 'Hey, we're gonna go get some drugs' or 'We're gonna go drop off some drugs.' He just gave me a lot of money to just go. 'You wanna go with me, I'll give you some money?' 'Sure!'"* When she said this "sure," her face broke out into a big smile and she sat up straighter, eyes lit up, remembering the joy of making easy money: all she had to do was sit in a car and take us to the lake. All she had to do was follow a don't ask, don't tell policy, and pretend she hadn't seen whatever it was she saw.

Living in El Paso was the priority for my mother so that my brother could go to school in English. Undocumented, her options in El Paso were to clean houses or work in nightlife. Putting emotions aside, which she's quite skilled at, the calculations were easy. Cleaning houses made little money even if you worked long hours every day because Mexican women crossed the border from Juarez to work at essentially Mexican prices. Dancing for tips at the strip club, on the other hand, offered more income and more freedom, both of which were invaluable as a single mother. Dancers only had to work three days a week, which meant she could stay home with us most days.

"It was okay, because it wasn't every day, even though I hated that job. I was embarrassed working there. I never liked it. Ay, no. There were some women, oooooh! They gave it their all. I never did. Once I'd made the money I wanted to make, I'd go to the back and not come out, play dumb. All I needed was $250 for rent and the light bill and a little bit of extra money. I got food stamps and Medicaid for you and your brother, and I also got a $92 check every month for you guys. Then they made it a nude club. It was topless when I started. When they made it a nude club, I hated it even more."

Working at night, she could walk my brother to school in the morning and stay home with us during the day. She also didn't have to find someone to care for us: she'd leave us at home to sleep, locking the door behind her after reminding us to be quiet and keep the lights off so the neighbor wouldn't know. She felt we were safest alone, and maybe she was right.

I am four years old, and sleeping by my brother, when we hear our mother's low whispers, calling our names. She has red lipstick on and smells of cigarette. As we fully awaken, she says, "Look what I brought you." She smiles, and I feel joy because she doesn't smile much. She's more prone to scowls than to smiles.

In her hands she is holding two VHS movies, *Hercules* for my brother and *Thumbelina* for me. My brother gets up right away to put *Hercules* in the VHS player. Once he is awake and going, his mind doesn't stop. I am just pleased my mother is back, even though she will now sleep for most of the morning.

This is my first memory. My mother coming home from work late at night, to that little place she rented for us for $250 a month. It is only through our interviews that I was able to place that memory in the context that we were living. Now that I can, her love, the ways in which she has guarded our innocence and fed our dreams, seems all the more remarkable. We did the math together of the years she spent working at a job she hated so she could raise us with more care—1996, '97, '98, until June 1999 when we drove to Alabama. That it was so many years pains me, as if my heart is being squeezed even as it grows. For my mother, it is a stretch of years that now seems like nothing, just a single bad memory tucked away in a corner of her heart, memories she doesn't see unless she wants to, to remember the sacrifices she has made for her children.

"When I was young, I wanted to have children and I wanted to have a family. That was my dream when I was a little girl. I wanted to be married and have a good husband. Seeing my father always cheat on my mother and beat her, I was never going to forgive someone for that. Your

brother's dad and I, we were going to build a family and everything. Then I found out he was cheating on me, and he tried to hit me once. I knew that the men that he would go out with were beating their wives and cheating on them all the time. Those women wouldn't leave. I thought, 'What the hell is wrong with them?' I told him I wasn't going to be that woman. I wasn't going to stand for that. I was young and naive, and suddenly, bam! I was so, so disappointed. It was like some switch turned on in me and I thought, 'I don't want anything.' Maybe that's where I learned that you shouldn't be in a relationship. Then all men just became someone I could get something out of. It wasn't the same anymore. I became a cynical person."

When her hope to have a loving husband disappeared, my mother chose to shut herself off and instead made the hard choice of raising us alone no matter the costs. "I always thought that I was so glad that I wasn't married because I saw how many children, they would go through their parents' fights and all that. I thought my children were more stable than all those children."

When she met my father, she had no hopes for a fairytale story, and in fact, my father was just like any other of the misogynist men she had encountered in her life. Nearing the end of our interview, she explained why she didn't speak of my father when I was a child. "I never wanted to tell you anything about your dad, nothing bad. Because what am I going to say to you? 'Oh, he lied to me . . .' There's nothing to say. That he lied? That he was married? I can make myself the victim, I can say bad things about him, but I'm not one of those. I also played my part. I always thought that I would poison your heart if I told you ugly things when you were a little girl. Why? What's the point? That's wrong to poison kids' hearts. It's not a burden they should be carrying."

My mother says she was a cynic by seeing men with eyes of interest, but I think she was an idealist, shielding us from a reality she rejected even as she endured it. There was no fairy tale about my father to uncover, but I witnessed my mother's magic listening to her weightlessly remember a crushing past while standing tall, stronger for the weight she's carried. She charted a course she'd never coursed to create our own type of fairy tale, making real a reality that seemed unreachable. In this special place that she created is where she raised me, so I could grow up to ask innocent questions with an unpoisoned heart.

For Circe

Lauren Hayes

How I love to be with you on the island of Aeaea
>Where we dance along the faces
>>Of jagged cliffs

And laugh carelessly into the wind
>Every time
>>We don't plunge to our deaths in the depths below

There is no beginning or end
>Only this
>>Green Infinity

Where our skin is forever scented with herbs

Our ears no longer ring with the screaming of coarse and vengeful pigs
>For we have taken all to slaughter
>>To make space for gentler beasts

We wash the gore from our pale limbs,
>Knowing (truly)
>>That this was the only way

A mercy, really

Now we gather our beloveds
      Furred, and feathered, and fleeced
            Wrap them in our shining strands as swaddled babes

And carry all home with us to dine on honey-sweet cream

At our feast.

Laundry

Esther Ra

Whenever I gather an armful of laundry from the dryer,
I bury myself in its fresh, fragrant warmth—a snowbank
of soft heat, a field of loose linen and lilies. This pleasure
feels almost decadent, extreme, when I consider how many
women in North Korea still hunch over frozen riverbeds
to beat their clothes clean. Although I still have my worries—
grades, interviews, cold calls, love—they pale
in the radiant shock of being a woman learning law
in America: free to ask questions and make mistakes, build a life
undefined by my people's pressure. In Bogotá, my sister
watches her friend's marble-eyed, broad-shouldered husky
bound across the sun-dipped grass, and she cries at the sight
of his freedom—a feeling she has just begun to fully experience,
and fears she will forget in Korea. What am I, if not my country's
sorrows? Like saying goodbye to a favorite ghost, I fear the day
I will no longer be haunted—by the long cold days on the bus
in the rain, surrounded by my people, crying with loneliness;
swinging at the playgrounds at night, watching the apartments
of my small city sparkle; the lamplit, hole-in-the-wall, unfamous
cafes; the solitary prayers; my mother's face. In class, a researcher
tells us about the survivors of Ireland's Magdalene laundries,

those prison-like buildings with gates topped with glass, where girls
were beaten and starved and worked to the bone. *It wasn't
the most vulnerable who were sent to those places,* she said—
*it was the strongest, the girls who talked back, who had voices,
who flirted.* Those who shone too brightly to be contained.
Asking them questions, drinking tea at their flats, she thought,
*That could have been me, a generation ago—I could have been
one of them.* I understand, because when North Korean women
told me their stories, I thought of my own mother, and sobbed.
My sister says, *We have our mother's blood in us, Esther.
We are lonely. We need men. We can't help it.* But no one
lights a lamp to cover it with a vessel, or hide it under a bed.
My sisters' souls flicker like candles that cannot be put out,
fingertips enveloped with light. Yesterday the sun was out,
and light streamed down like a waterfall; I climbed up
on a bench and threw out my arms, gathered warmth
to my neck like fresh laundry. A friend walking by
shouted out, *You look majestic!* I was breathing unhindered
in this—my one body. I was blazing with light. I was free.

In the Middle of Nowhere

Rosie Cohan

"Mt. Fitz Roy? Really!" asked the young travel agent in Buenos Aires dressed in a tight leather skirt and three-inch stilettos.

"The wind is often biting. It can rain or snow at any time. If you aren't climbers, or trekkers, you will be in the middle of nowhere with nothing to do."

I detected a slight smirk as she talked. She probably thought I was too old and chubby to trek on one of the most technically challenging mountains in the world. But, the otherworldly appearance of jagged Mt. Fitz in Patagonia was ensconced in my memory ever since I first saw pictures of it in the late 1980s. Thirty years later, I finally had both the time and money to see it in person.

My friend Arlene, four years older than I am, is thin and in good shape. She shot me one of those "are you crazy" looks.

"I don't want to be miserable stranded on some mountain in freezing rain and cold. You can go on your own if you want." Turning to the travel agent Arlene asked, "Where else would you recommend?"

Arlene's words ignited my own insecurities. I had the will, but would the body follow? I was at the age of senior moments, and my degenerating knee and back were reinforced with cortisone. Although I didn't feel old in my mind and heart, the body doesn't lie.

I looked up the term "trek" when researching Mt. Fitz Roy near El Chaltén, the trekking capital of Argentine Patagonia. The definition, "an arduous journey," flashed neon in my mind. In response to peer pressure and my own self-doubts, I reluctantly dropped Mt. Fitz Roy from our itinerary. Yet, the mythic image of the slate-gray, flat-faced mountain continued to call to me.

A week later, we were in El Calafate to see the colossal Perito Moreno. A ranger told us it is one of the only glaciers in the world that is not receding and they don't know why. We approached the glacier by boat and heard what was like a lightning crack and thunder rumbling under the cloudless cerulean sky. Two large icebergs broke off and fell into the lake looking like giant white-robed sumo wrestlers crashing into the water. They submerged and bounced out of the water gasping for air, bobbing several times and then became part of the growing meringue-peaked ice field. Cobalt-blue spider veins were running through the glacier's aqua iridescent face. We were told the deeper the penetration of light on the ice, the darker the color becomes.

We hiked on a series of wooden walkways examining various angles of the enormous glacier. Sitting on a bench eating our lunch, a tall, ethereal man with long white hair falling down his shoulders appeared and asked if he could join us. He was in his late sixties and was Swiss. He told us he was going to El Chaltén that night by bus to trek Mt. Fitz Roy.

"We were told it would be too difficult for us to trek there," I said with disappointment in my voice.

He looked surprised. "Oh, you shouldn't miss it. It is only about two hours away by bus. My friends say trekking at Mt. Fitz Roy is the highlight of Patagonia."

Arlene's eyebrows arched as she looked up from her sandwich. "You aren't worried about terrible weather?"

"I know the weather is unpredictable and it's a difficult trek. But there is an easier trail you can take for the day with some spectacular viewpoints of Fitz Roy. It starts near a waterfall. Why would you miss seeing one of the most beautiful places on earth?"

He then waved goodbye. Looking back at us he yelled, "Hope to see you tomorrow at El Chaltén." Then he disappeared.

My inner compass, which has always led me to my most memorable travel experiences, switched back on and pointed toward Mt. Fitz Roy. I decided I would go there, even if I had to go alone. After listening to the Swiss man, Arlene changed her mind and agreed to go.

That evening, I booked a van to take us to El Chaltén the next morning. I had forgotten that the Alps were the Swiss man's point of reference when he made his emphatic recommendation.

Bundled up in layers, we waited in the cold morning air for the van. Ribbons of gold painted onto the indigo sky gave way to the bright rising sun. The glaciers in the distance stood like sunrise sentries reflecting the rose and orange clouds. The van arrived and we joined twelve other sleepy adventurers. Some wore Patagonia clothing imprinted with their emblem of Mt. Fitz Roy. All had the glow of youth, except for a gray-haired couple who said they were taking a boat to see the mountain from the lake.

Traveling along legendary Route 40, which parallels the Andes, I looked for young Che on his motorcycle, or maybe Butch Cassidy. But all I saw were a few cars and trucks. Then three guanacos (Argentine llamas) appeared on the side of the road next to my window. Their huge doe eyes widened with surprise when they saw me staring at them. In a second, they turned and ran so you could only see their chestnut and white–striped backs vibrating up the side of the hillside.

We began to climb in elevation. The variegated blue Lago Argentino was in the background. The scenery changed from golden brown hills punctuated with silver bushes to mountains covered in trees dressed in autumnal glory. After about an hour, the steel-like, serrated peaks of Mt. Fitz Roy came into view amid a swirl of mist and clouds. It looked like a storm might break at any moment above the mountain. I avoided looking at Arlene, who was then probably regretting her decision to come.

We finally passed through the town of El Chaltén founded in 1985 as an Argentine outpost so Chile would not control all of Patagonia. The one-road town contained varnished log cabins and Easter candy–colored A-frame houses. It was gone in a blink as we approached a wooded area. The driver stopped and gave instructions for our pickup six hours later.

Hearing rushing water, we hiked on a short path surrounded by El Calafate trees, holly-like bushes with reddish-purple berries. Mini rainbows were playing hide and seek on the tall waterfall near a few of Mt. Fitz Roy's trailheads. On a wooden, two-dimensional map that didn't reflect the topography, Arlene and I identified what we thought was the trail the Swiss man had described.

Arlene said, "It doesn't look that far, maybe four miles." But she hadn't quite mastered the conversion of meters to miles.

"Piece of cake," I said, relieved. "We hike four miles all the time at home."

The "easy" trail was an almost vertical, rough, rocky path close to the mountain's edge. It had turned into an unusually sunny fall day. There was no biting wind, but no breeze either. After about ten minutes, I had peeled off most of my layers and was sweating profusely. I began to ache as I looked up to what seemed to be an endless ascent. Using the pretense of wanting to enjoy the view, I stopped every ten minutes so I wouldn't hyperventilate. The pain in my back began traveling down my hip and eventually down my leg. My right knee was crackling with each step up the rock-strewn path. I took a pain pill to help me continue the upward ordeal.

Despite her initial concerns to take the trip, Arlene was making the climb like a goat and was far ahead of me. She is tall and thin, and I am a short endomorph who is always starting my diet *manana*. She would eventually wait for me and try to encourage me forward by offering me chocolate calcium chews and hard candies.

I struggled upward. I tripped and grabbed onto a prickly bush, which broke my fall and saved me from dangling over the cliff. In the process, I skinned my decrepit knees and my chin bled from falling onto the sharp rocks lining the path. I carried Band-Aids and stopped the bleeding from my knees and chin. I sat on the ground picking small thorns from my hands. Arlene called down to me, and not wanting her to see me cry, I yelled for her to go ahead and I would catch up. Alone, I sat dejected, not a victim of the mountain but of my own self-recriminations.

To add insult to injury, a group of young backpackers, loaded with packs larger than they were, sped by me. "Do you need any help?" one cute young girl asked, noticing my bandages and my slumped body and sad demeanor.

I shook my head and said no thank you. As they continued on, I heard one of the guys say, "Wonder what she is doing up here?"

I wondered too. Maybe it was time to face the reality that I can't do the things I used to do when I was younger. Maybe I should have just taken a boat ride on the lake while drinking maté, or better yet Malbec. Self-doubt began to constrict my breathing even more. My legs vibrated, my balance was unsteady, and my confidence was shot. I was ready to quit.

Arlene was waiting for me on the next ridge but came back down to me to see what was wrong.

"I don't know if I can really make it," I said with tears welling up.

The look of concern on her face betrayed her doubts also, but she tried to be encouraging. "You can make it. I think the hardest part is probably behind us. We should reach the top of this trail soon. I am tired too. Let's rest and have a snack. You will feel better. Look at the magnificent view below us."

Chomping on almonds and an apple, I swallowed some of my self-pity. As I stared down into the valley, the scene below looked like an art gallery filled with impressionist and abstract paintings. A distant mineral-rich, turquoise river snaked through a blend of rose and chocolate swirled mountains punctuated with pointillist trees in the fall spectrum. Brilliant orange, yellow, and cobalt-blue butterflies darted across this natural canvas leaving tiny animated splashes of color. Instead of rain and snow, we had an iridescent blue sky with pillows of clouds bouncing by. I wondered if the pain pill I had taken earlier was really a hallucinogenic.

When one looks at an artwork, it can change your perspective. Looking at nature's artwork, I focused on how far I had actually come up the mountain, and not on how far I had left to go. My aching muscles began to soften, my breathing slowed, and my will to finish the climb returned. Meditating on the glorious view, nature helped to soothe and rejuvenate me.

I began to give myself some credit. If I hadn't tried this trek, it would have become a "woulda, shoulda, or coulda" missed opportunity. There were other times I passed up incredible experiences because of what other people told me. As a result, I've found out that regret sometimes can be more debilitating than physical pain.

Although steep, by taking the climb step by step with slow, persistent effort, I thought I could continue on. A tape in my head played my mother's voice repeating her favorite saying, "Persistency wins." She had lived until ninety-seven years old, so she knew what she was talking about.

Feeling determined, I pulled my bedraggled body up, found a branch to use as a walking stick, and started up the mountain again. We soon approached a point where we were face to face with Fitz Roy's serrated slate peaks. The clouds had lifted, and we had a rare view of the steely gray mountain naked against the brilliant blue sky. A deep reverence fell over me. I now understood why in many cultures people believe that God dwells on mountain tops.

A bit farther up, we conquered the top of the trail. There was a small, pebbled beach edging the glassy aqua lake, Laguna Capri. Quietly devouring our bag lunches, serenaded by the gentle lapping of waves while sunrays danced off the water, I looked up to see just above us one giant white-accented black Andean condor spreading its enormous wings. I imagined it a sign to keep spreading my own wings.

Tired, but refreshed, we began the descent to El Chaltén. Huge boulders lined the path decorated with engraved gold lichen hieroglyphics, which I am sure contained ancient secrets. Distant red, mushroom-like formations deepened in the afternoon light. We reached the town after about five hours of trekking, instead of the three hours the trail usually takes others. Another lesson learned from Mt. Fitz Roy—experiencing the journey is the goal, not the time involved.

I was exhausted, but the pains in my back, knees, and other aching parts were dulled by feeling a combination of relief, exhilaration, and accomplishment. As we walked to the van pickup spot, a man with streaming white hair flying in the wind ran down from an upper trail. He waved his arms and was shouting to us.

"I didn't think you would really come." It was the Swiss man from Perito Moreno.

"Did you think you were talking to some wimps?" I teased. "Thank you so much for encouraging us to come."

We gave him big hugs. Meeting him again seemed more than a coincidence. Over a cold beer in one of the four bars on the one-block town, I described my challenges and how the power of nature led me from doubt and despair to perseverance and reverence.

As we left El Chaltén, we stopped for one last view of Fitz Roy. The sun was beginning to set. The triumph of the day radiated on my face in the van's rearview mirror. The soft glow at dusk seemed to camouflage my crow's feet and wrinkles.

I keep a picture of Fitz Roy on my desktop. It reminds me to follow what my heart tells me no matter what others say or my own doubts and fears. If I don't succeed, I must at least try. To try is in itself a success.

Mt. Fitz Roy remains a symbol that experiences in nature can be challenging and treacherous, yet they have the power to create, restore, and inspire. The forbidding mountain is a symbol that sometimes the middle of nowhere is just the somewhere you were meant to be.

Re: My Continued Tardiness

Mary Paulson

This time I admit, had nothing to do with
trains or timetables or tourists
blocking the way. There was just really,
sincerely nothing to wear, nothing
that accurately represented the *je* in my
je ne sais quoi. Was I to misrepresent
myself? Make a mockery of
my truth, more to the point, dare I
go to work ill clothed and unprepared?

The day began like any other, by
waking and first things first—spiriting away
any visible and emotional ennui
with my own combination of sheep's blood
and L'Oreal cosmetics. This is essential.
One must be fully composed before
descending into the subways or facing
the throngs crowding 42nd Street. It is
incumbent upon me to achieve a state of calm,
warrior-readiness before

I make any excursions outside
the walls of this apartment. Only then
can I hope to frankly be, the very
best employee I can be. It was only
during my last-minute preparations that I became
frozen with indecision. A spear?
Too conspicuous. Cross-bow? Too bulky.
Poison arrow had been my first choice
but accessories have always
been a problem for me and while the arrow

was a solid choice, it occurred to me
too late that some sharpened bit of
ancient obsidian would surely
wear its way right through my pantyhose so
I had to rule it out. What then?
A handgun? Too pedestrian. A shiv? Too
prison-specific. Anything explosive, of course,
was out of the question. Not only is it
terribly gauche, it's far too reminiscent of the tragic
finale of Melrose Place and a difficult
memory I'd rather not revisit—

It happened a week before my college
graduation. I had just drunk a despicable tea
of Psilocybin mushrooms—my first—with several
of my closest drug-taking friends. After
waiting thirty minutes for *something* to happen
and when nothing did, I got bored,
jumped into my VW Golf and headed
out to a nearby lawn party,

I won't bore you with the details, except to say
I forgot how to drive a car halfway
to the lawn party, parked as it were, on the
lawn, and stood in line with what
appeared to be, a host of
horrifying little pigs in white halter tops.
By the time I made it back
to my friends, they were fixated on the TV
and the explosive finale. It was then,

I felt everyone's hostility directed
Squarely at me, because, as I found out later
I was wearing a short black dress, which,
spiritually speaking, was in direct conflict with
the themes of summer and the others'
uber cool white T-shirts. Ever since,
I've taken my wardrobe choices
rather seriously, carefully assessing my
accessory to outfit to lipstick ratio—and I'm sorry to say

that any of those weapons would have clashed
appallingly with the midi linen dress
and Armani blazer I had already chosen.
It was a shame really because the Jimmy Choos
accentuated my hourglass figure and
the whole arrangement could be easily
turned from day-time smart to evening chic just
by switching out the earrings. Still,
it was obvious to me that despite the time
restraints, I had no choice but to re-think literally
EVERYTHNG—and build my clothing
choices around a whole new look.

Oh no! How silly of me, that wasn't it
at all. I remember now. It was a transportation issue,
after all. It happened when the cross-town bus
Destined Never To Arrive never arrived. Can someone
tell me please, is "Bus Stop" a label bus drivers
frankly avoid? Is it the supposed entitlement of passengers
that think they can hop on wherever there's a sign?
Honestly, I would have been better off riding a donkey,
but in this city, who can afford one?

After a Long Walk, I Talk to Myself

Kayla Heinze

When you arrive at the end
　　you will be overcome.

It's not important with what,
　　let it happen.

Hear the trees applaud;
　　feel the wind at your back

still pointing the way.

There will be grand spectacles
　　to mark this special place.

I ask only that you revel
　　in this strange family of life

with its destructive greed
　　and ancient moral lessons.

Wonder at the cathedrals.
　　Wonder at the sacred truths—

those ones you found right here, in your bones.

When you have made it to the end
     of something difficult, painful

or delightfully strenuous
      find time

to set your body down, to let your spirit loose.
     Dancing on the altar of your own fire.

Those splendid, holy flames
     they have burned a path for you

and the journey is just beginning.

The Procedure

Molly Murfee

Taking my flip flops off at the threshold of willows, I squish through ground velveted in chartreuse moss, water from the lake moistening the hillocks impregnated with Beavers' trails, heading to their juiciest cache. I hunker down in my spot on the edge of The Lake, like so many mornings, strategically ooching into the tall grass between the serrated leaves of the Bog Birch and the white flower clusters of the Hemlock. Giant cerulean Dragonflies land in succession on the dried branch in front of me, chasing, mating. And then I hear it, the bull Elk bugling from somewhere in the willow forest, the high metallic soar falling into a series of grunts.

There was a time, many thousands of years ago in my native culture, when there was no distinction between the sacred and the secular. The lake you walked past on your walk every day. The very act of walking. The land itself was a goddess incarnate, as were lakes, rivers, mountains. The crow. The raven. The rabbit. Animals spoke with humans, serving as mediators between them, the deities, and the Otherworld. Everything had a spirit. All were sacred. European archeologists have found thousands of votives across the Celtic nations at the bottoms of such watery portals, offered in reverence, and in plea. Magical things happened in places such as these. These very real places. It was here where poets divined meaning, wisdom, and inspiration, the landscape as symbol, like a secret language deciphered through code.

I lie back, spread out, allow the sun to drip into my pores like warm honey. There is something about this day that tingles, like it often does in the fall. Everything glowing gold and red. Vibrating. Throbbing. The cloudless, sapphire sky presses me warmly into the earth. My skin flushes. I come to this spot again and again, a ritual to begin the day. An embrace. I open to this world. Take it inside of me. Air into my lungs, water to my veins, flesh to my mouth. We are the same, are one. Elements and minerals reflecting blood and bone. I accept it all—the breathtaking beauty, the pain and the poison. Tell me, I whisper to the womb of water lapping at my toes, how do I speak your language, tap into the infinite, creative soul of this world, translate your messages for the greater good? What is it you need to have heard?

Two weeks later I am bleeding.

They say you are post-menopausal once you have moved through a cycle of thirteen moons, a full year, without menstruating. I was coming up on two. I call my gynecologist. She immediately sends me to ultrasound. This isn't normal, she says. We need to act quickly. I make the appointment. Wait days. Worrying, fretting, trying not to envision the worst-case scenario. A dear friend had just been through this. Her hysterectomy to remove the cancer they found in her uterus began with post-menopausal bleeding. She went in to check it out. Within days she was in surgery, then chemotherapy, radiation. I try to push this from my mind. I don't call her back when she serendipitously leaves a message on my machine, just checking in, saying hi.

I have the pelvic ultrasound on a Saturday in a room shaded from the sun. Watch the cloudy picture shift and move as she glides the instrument over my belly. The technician clicks and highlights. We chat about housing.

I wait more days.

When my doctor calls with the results I'm not at home. "Call me back," she says on the machine, "soon." I do. But she is seeing other patients.

Another day passes.

"You have a lot of fibroids," she reports when we finally connect. "If they are on the inside of the cavity of your uterus they could bleed. But there is also something blocking your cervical canal. We can't tell what it is. It could be a fibroid, or a polyp, but whatever it is, it has to go. I need to do a biopsy to make sure that's all it is, and I can't do a biopsy with this blockage in the way. You need to schedule an appointment with the hospital. It's a minor procedure—outpatient, you'll go home the same day—but you have to go under anesthesia. You'll be having a hysteroscopy and a D&C."

I've never been under anesthesia, never had a "procedure," major or minor. My hands shake as I call her assistant to begin the process; my voice shakes as I answer questions of availability. I make it for as soon as possible. I try to focus on my doctor's words, "it could be a fibroid, or a polyp," but the "we can't tell" keeps ringing in my mind like a toll. I try to stay off the internet. Practice meditations pulling golden, healing light into my uterus. Envision it as a garden, full of flowers. A waterfall running through, washing away anything that might harm me.

Once in my twenties I got my palm read. "Oh, wow," the fortune teller says, "I've never seen this before. Your life line is completely broken in half, but then it continues. You live a long life, but something happens in the middle." She looks up at me and smiles. "You survive." Then, I wondered in what form. Now, I study it, notice a tendril of a crease that connects the two halves then continues up the center. I close my hand into a fist and try not to think about it. During the season of the Autumn Equinox I pull the Uruz rune, while paused at the apex of a bridge arching over The River, into which waters of The Lake ultimately filter. It is the rune of the Elk, indicating a rite of passage, and a reminder the untamed powers of creativity are not without danger. It is associated with the color red and the element of the earth. Yet it is also a symbol of physical health, strength, endurance, and survival. The ability to heal, and protect the psyche from trauma. The presence of vital lifeforce. I focus on this.

Women's bodies are sensitive. We take on the world, harbor its ills. Poisons in our air, soil, water impact us deeply, take up residence in our uterus, our ovaries, our breasts. Our life-giving centers. Passing them on to our babies. We are like canaries in a coal mine. Sensitive. Attentive. Intuitive.

It has been this way since the dawn of humanity, although at times, now, forgotten. Women's ability to give birth connects us to the even more powerful life-giving capacities of the entire universe. Our bodies contain a mystery connected to the most profound mysteries of the cosmos. The wonderments of female fertility and biology dominated religious and artistic thought for the first 200,000 years of human existence. Our supreme role became that of cultural producers, mothers, and prime communicators with the spirit world. As creators we were revered as the very essence, the very symbol, of creativity. God was known first as a woman.

The first religion was a sexual-spiritual one, a celebration of cosmic ecstasy. Women's religious practices were rife with art and magic, tools to access the language of trees or birds or beasts as incarnations of the Goddess. These were ecstatic women, shamans and seers who entered trance states, responsible for keeping the energy channels open and flowing between individuals, the group, and the great cosmic source. It was a trend that continued to the Celtic world, many thousands of years later, where women still served as the communicators and mediators between the Otherworld and humans, where sacred, sexual marriages bound the land and the king in a consequential contract of stewardship and subsequent abundance. Sex was the source of life.

I return to The Lake. The womb waters with the island navel, where the tree of the axis mundi grows. Like many cultures across time and space, the Celts believed in a sacred center of the world, upheld by a sacred tree, a pillar supporting the heavens, and therefore connecting the threefold cosmos of earth, sky, and sea. After the Grandmother Heron, a creature flying and wading between worlds of air and water, gets her fill of fish on the edges of The Lake, she comes to rest in the tops of this tree, as if surveying her domain. For beneath the surface of lakes such as these, the Otherworld lives. The home of gods and goddesses, spirits and ancestors, magical beings and cauldrons of rebirth. For the Greeks of a similar era, water on earth was conceived by the elemental god Oceanus, one of the sons of the Earth Goddess, Gaia. Oceanus was also the cosmic river surrounding Earth, marking the boundary of the known and the unknown. His are liminal places of transition. It is a passageway. A portal. I wonder what she can see below the surface.

By all ancient accounts, I am in the presence of divinity.

Except.

What I know is that the muck beneath the surface is thick with heavy metals, waste runoff from the mining days. If only you don't disturb it, they say, all will be well. I watch Beaver yanking aquatic grasses up from the bottom, shoving wads of green strands in her mouth for an evening snack. Diving Ducks disappearing underneath, returning with beaks and bellies full of Snails. The herd of Elk wading and swimming and drinking on The Lake's eastern edge. Grandmother Heron stalking fish among the reeds. And I wonder . . .

The Celtic Otherworld was an ambiguous place. It was beautiful, rich, brimming with abundance and gifts. It could also be dangerous, leaving you either wounded or in wonderment. The metaphors and symbols emanating from it were alive, moving, ever-changing. Life-giving Sovereignty Goddesses like the promiscuous and powerful Mórrigan also had shadow sides—terrifying, chaotic, and unpredictable. They could brew both storms and sickness. They could conjure death or predict its coming. Protect or annihilate. Creation was always preceded by a necessary destruction.

Kneeling in the grass on the bank of The Lake, I plead. "Take it back. I'm only a small human. My body cannot house these ills. I will fight for you, I promise, but I cannot take on this sickness." Abort. Abort.

I feel guilty. The Earth bears so much, so much disease in her body. So much violation. So much depletion. She carries it. I cannot. It is too much. "I don't want to see you shoulder the world," a woman in my writing group says in a feedback session. I'm embarrassed I can't do more.

I'm in my pre-op stall, stripped to my gown with the opening in the back, an IV drip of saline in my veins, canary yellow socks with grippy nubbins on my feet, a bright red band warning of my penicillin allergy on my wrist. A series of professionals cycle through—my pre-op nurse who is cheery and tells me how great I'm doing, the nurse who will be in the operating room with me and smiles reassuringly, the nurse anesthetist who is sharp and focused and asks about my history of heart palpitations, my doctor who answers my questions about my recent covid exposure, and if it was a threat in any kind of way. Then they all leave. I wait.

"I want to go home," I sob to my partner, Mark, who sits at my bedside holding the hand without the IV and all the identification wrist bands. I'm terrified. Of the procedure. Of the anesthesia. Of my penicillin allergy and heart palpitations. Of the results. The inevitability of it all is excruciating. I know women have endured worse, more, but there is nothing about this that feels minor to me. I feel like a wimp.

The nurse anesthetist and operating room nurse return. "Time to go." The latter smiles as she wheels me out, the former preparing a needled cocktail to go into my IV. The last thing I remember I'm looking up at the operating room lights. The nurse anesthetist instructs me about the translucent green mask she is lowering over my mouth and nose. My doctor comes to the head of the gurney and looks down on me reassuringly. The mask doesn't feel like it's fitting right. In my growing haze I try to adjust it, I think. Then nothing.

It sounds like a convocation of angels gathered in a circle around me, talking. As my eyes flutter open my gynecologist asks me if I know who she is. I respond with the correct answer. She leaves. Then the pain. The operating room nurse is querying about pain numbers, adjusting pain medication through multiple rounds, then cajoling me to sit up. I don't want to. "How did my heart do?" I manage to whisper. "Your heart did great." "Was it a polyp or a fibroid?" I feel I can barely muster the energy to push the words out. She leans in, smiling, always smiling, trying to break through the fog. "Neither." She is nodding, her face close. "It was just a piece of flesh. Your uterus is healthy." She brings in my clothes, begins unhooking my IV. I'm told to take Tylenol. Mark drives me home. I immediately curl up in the bed in a fetal position and return to sleep.

A pound of flesh.

I have been through a portal, a rite of passage. The Wise Elder Woman always said it was so—modern-day surgeons, nurses, and anesthesiologists as shamans, the process of an operation the shamanic journey. I didn't understand before. Now I do. Down and down through the dark cone, this funneling to a pinpoint in time when all stands still. A place of healing in the blackness, the unknown, the unconscious. Without artificial assistance my lungs would have ceased to expand and contract. My heart beat, but still it feels like a tiny death. A place of nothingness. A place beyond the River of Forgetfulness. It was only a brief sip, but enough to know, and then not.

I creep on hands and knees from darkness to light through the other side of the hourglass. Something removed, something causing a leak of lifeforce when I should be gathering in, something I could not expunge on my own. A shedding. When I look at myself in the mirror there is something in my eyes I hadn't seen before. A darkness around the edges. A deepening. Some sort of sign I'd been somewhere. The Void. For the ancient Greeks this great Void was called Chaos, a dark nigredo, the origin of everything. I feel soft and tender, vulnerable, like the chartreuse caterpillars munching away in my garden.

My belly is still aching and cramping and bleeding. I place my hands there to warm it, to question, to listen. What is it I hold in this pristine place I envisioned as ripe and smooth, plump and spacious, that never bore a child, but now bore this clump of flesh? What emotions might reside here, residue of something unresolved, forcing attention, and a way out?

I wonder if this was perhaps some innate sadness, of not having done what was biologically expected. My rebellious nature hates to admit I have always longed to do the right thing. But it doesn't quite ring true; I never had that irrefutable maternal instinct. When I realized I was entering menopause I stopped for a moment. I remember looking out the window and thinking. What was always a choice was now becoming not one. That was different. I squinted into the sunlight, evaluated the branches of the subalpine fir harboring broad-tailed Hummingbirds and white-crowned Sparrows, and continued about my day. Nevertheless, a uterus with a purpose unfulfilled, so society says. Perhaps it was some sort of biological final hurrah of trying to do something before the dark silence truly set in.

I wonder what I shoved into my womb, becoming the fibroids in its walls—the parental controls that didn't serve me, the relationships that didn't serve me, the jobs that didn't serve me, the cultural constructs that didn't serve me, my own mental constructs that didn't serve me. What are fibroids but a knotting, twisting, amassing, holding, hardening. I think to the recent flare of inflammation in my hands— again a heating and retaining, stiffening, guarding my body against injury and threats. The pandemic. Climate catastrophe. Financial uncertainty. Fear. I think to my nighttime tooth grinding, ruthlessly chewing my own mouth. The resolute bracing and frustration around expectations that don't feed my soul. The eternal to-do list of society's demands I care nothing about. The forced inflexibility of it all. Anger.

A D&C is the procedure used for abortions and miscarriages. A scraping away of something that is not right. I think to the power and fear women's wombs have exacted over men throughout the centuries, and therefore men's retaliation of control. How women's bodies and their ability to give birth have been used as political ploys.

The patriarchal god that overtook the matrifocal religions was not one of matter and the Earth, but of spirit. As the tradition spread across Europe it became apparent if the goal was to dominate with a singular deity, spirits and divinity couldn't live in the lakes, mountains, trees, and animals. The sacred stuff of the universe was summarily separated from nature and put somewhere distant into the unknowable and unreachable sky.

Women's direct and intimate connection to these forces came into question. The ecstatic tie had to be broken if the new religion was to take hold, and it was done in large part through women's sexuality and the very physicality of their wombs. As is often the case in such takeovers, the goddesses of the old religion became demons of the next. Women who clung to the ancient traditions were deemed a threat, and therefore subjugated and marginalized. Sex was no longer a path to the divine, but a definitive obstacle. God could no longer be known, only thought about.

When St. Patrick landed on the Emerald Isle it was rife with Sovereignty Goddesses, sensual, female place spirits who were the land. These divine women were free, having sex with their chosen in exchange for a pledge to protect the earth, swearing on the sun, moon, and wind. Abundance traded for stewardship. Multiple partners were the norm. Kings and chiefs didn't always keep their pledge and were summarily dethroned.

The sacredness of the elements was called into question. Gone became the days an individual could directly access the divine. Now it had to be mediated by a priest, male; women weren't allowed. And there were rules.

You can't have a patriarchy if you don't know who the father is, and women couldn't possibly be in charge of who got to rule, so in the interests of growing the new religion and keeping a certain king, powerful women with multiple partners just wouldn't do. Birth must be regulated. Virgins became revered. If sex was a confessional sin, priests held the control over salvation. The Old Testament had already played a heavy hand in the Garden of Eden, birthing pains and subordination as punishment for a woman causing the fall of the entirety of humankind. Shame over one's body. Guilt over one's actions. Women were not to be trusted. They cavorted with Snakes. Monogamy was instated. Cultural codes mandating that sex and birth were only to be had between a married man and a wife, hierarchical stratification dictating who exactly the pairing couple could be. Premarital sex was a sin winning you a ticket to hell. Assure the birth line. Growing a religion didn't just depend on converts, it could depend on sheer quantity. Ban abortion. Ban contraception. Pregnancies forced in the name of numbers. Menarche and menses were dirty, disgusting things. Embarrassing. No one even talked about menopause. Women's connection to nature was deemed of the devil and was thus severed. Threatened with death by fire or drowning.

We hold this.

So does the Earth.

It is our first wound.

The severance of our intimate relationship to a sacred and animate nature.

The eradication of a woman's values and subsequent demands of care, nurturance, and responsibility to the land.

Of being forced into a certain way. Our manner of knowing and connecting demonized.

My gynecologist tells me fibroids impact 80 percent of today's women. I find it no wonder.

We have given our pound of knotted flesh. It is time to write a new story.

The womb is an emotional center. Recent studies connect it to our memory. I wonder just how deep this memory goes. "It's not like getting operated on your toe," I tell Mark, as I pad about the house, confounded by the utter exhaustion I feel.

In Eastern faith traditions such as Hinduism, the womb is the home of the second chakra, an energy center holding our creativity, sensuality, pleasure, and joy. It is called Svadhisthana, translated as "one's own dwelling," associated with water, and ruled by the goddess Parvati.

Daughter of the Father Himalaya, sister to the River Ganga, Parvati is the benevolent goddess of love and devotion, and one of the many manifestations of the primordial divine feminine energy known as Shakti. She is the mother of all creation, and so also, naturally, the goddess of power and energy—untamed, unchecked, and chaotic. A shapeshifter of sorts, she takes on a multitude of incarnations, according to her mood, and is therefore the progenitor of all other goddesses. As such, she is not only the kind and compassionate Parvati, renowned for her beauty; when provoked she is also Kali, the destroyer, transformer, and goddess of time and change. From Kali come all primal energies. She is the dark void that births the universe, and into which everything dissolves back into. In yet another mood Parvati takes the face of Durga, the warrior goddess, slaying demons.

The womb. Women.

It's a theme seen in ancient cultures across the globe and throughout time, over and over and over—the goddesses who bring forth life and abundance are also the ones who bring forth transitions, death. They stand with us at the crossroads. Greek goddesses Hecate, Demeter, and Rhea. The Celtic Mórrigan. It was the Greek goddess Night who, with Darkness, begot brightness and Day. The two forces are interdependent on one another.

This obstruction. In the end my doctor didn't know exactly what it was. No fibroid. No polyp. And, after the pathology report, the diagnosis of no cancer. My whole body aches from the sustained tension I've held over the past five weeks. I am grateful, relieved, but do not experience an immediate flush of release. I feel as if I've been through some sort of ordeal. Joined a tribe of women who share this experience, others like it. My uterus had done something, produced something. I leave my doctor's office in a startled dream.

She had offered a few potential explanations. Perhaps, she speculated, the muscular wall of the uterus, now without the normal protective lining it had come to know for over four decades, made it raw enough to bleed. A new era, without its soft armored cushion. Apt,

I think. I am sensing this upcoming phase of life is not for the faint of heart.

Or, she told me, I had a very thin endometrial lining, "a weakly proliferative pattern," the pathology report said, created by some lingering reservoir of estrogen. This could have been the culprit, as I tried to shed it, like toilet paper on your shoe.

I think again of all those wrong people, jobs, relationships, cultural codes, and situations. So many tossing their own agendas into this vessel they don't own. Becoming obstructions to birthing my own ambitions, my own flow blocked by a constant caretaking. I dreamt about it once. The first frame someone crying, "Help me, help me." The second with another demanding, "Look at me, look at me." Both times I diverted from my own path, my own direction, to attend to the needs of others. Creative energy and impulse therefore dead-ending, blocked, dammed, into all the wrong expenditures of my space and time. Distracted. Misdirected. Put aside. I permitted others' dreams, desires, or demands to line up in the queue before mine, as women are so often wont to do, secretly sequestering anger and resentment in my body as I went along. I allowed it. Made the flesh myself. Like a pearl around a grain of intruding sand.

The climacteric for a woman indicates the most intense years of menopause. In a decade-long process, or more, it aptly names those few years most immediately before and after the actual cessation of menses. This has been a bodily rhythm she has known her entire adult life. In the middle of immense physical upheaval her moons stop. The blood stops. The crescendo has arrived. The word comes from the Greek word *klimaktēr*, a "rung of a ladder." In botany it is the stage of a fruit's ripening.

It has indeed been a climax—experiencing my climacteric in the midst of the pandemic, in the midst of the environmental disasters of climate change. The existential crisis of us all spilling down into the dark funnel together. All as one. And as a writer, trying to make sense of the flooding, burning, sleepless mess, every bit of it scorching every pore of my body, fear and anxiety like live wires falling into the surging, muddy deluge.

I thought I was done. That it was going to subside. But now this flesh a tear, a giving, no, a taking. "A payment or penalty exacted to fulfill a deal or punishment," says Merriam-Webster of the proverbial pound. No matter of its impacts or consequences. Something someone feels they have a right to extract, just happy about the pretty pearl.

And my heart—just fluttering and fluttering—knowing none of it is right. It's not in sync, we're not in sync, not in rhythm, it's not a heart's choice.

And so, the tooth-grinding frustration.

The withholding inflammation, the fear to move, the desire to protect, trying to heal.

The shedding of this skin was the final release of mothering the miniscule that is not mine.

Metaphors hang like plump pomegranates. I pluck them fervently in my descent. Ravenous for any nourishment of sense-making.

Two weeks to the day before I began to bleed, in the pulse of a new moon, I had a dream. I am walking down a dirt road in a deciduous forest in the evening twilight. There is a blockade, reflective orange and white indicating a closure. Behind it, coiled and raring, is a mythically gigantic Snake, as high as a house. She is a brushed pink and peach, like the eyelash vipers I learned of in Costa Rica. I evaluate her colossal head. It looks to be rounded, but I know, in the dream, this can change. It does. The Snake pops out the sides of her head like an arrow, and it is then I know she is deadly. She is watching me. I slink through the barricade anyway, hoping she doesn't notice my growing proximity as I attempt to sidestep past her, frantically running backwards so I can keep an eye on her when she does. She is gaining on me, chomping and chomping with giant fangs, missing me by mere inches. Finally, I turn my back, running with all of my might.

For Hindus, the divine, cosmic feminine energy coiled at the base of the spine is called Kundalini, represented by a Snake. Summoned through a practitioner's meditating and chanting, the serpentine energy winds up the spine through all seven chakras, leading to spiritual awakening. In the ancient Near East the Snake was closely associated with the Goddess, representing or adorning her, serving as mediator between her and humans. Ninhursag, the Sumerian Mother Goddess, seen most prevalently in the third and second millennia BCE, was the creator of all living things, including humans, whom she formed out of clay and the blood of a god. She is one of the earliest known and named representations of a Mother Earth Goddess, her worship found in physical evidence dating back to 4500 BCE. Her symbol was a figure like the Greek Omega, indicative of the womb. She was often depicted as a Snake.

The Snake was thus a symbol of life and creation, fertility and sexuality. Because she hibernated in the underworld throughout winter, reemerging in the spring, because she shed her skin, she was seen as a symbol of death and rebirth, the turning of one form into another, and therefore hope and wisdom. She was a nondualistic creature, having the simultaneous capacity for both good and evil. Like the humans. Like the gods.

Her venom is both poison and antidote.

There is a part of menopause that is a death. A shedding of a past. And then, a recreation. An awakening to a new self. A continuing in a new form. What must be born before we die? What must die for it to be born?

The procedure was like a ruthless ripping off of the Band-Aid, clearing me finally of all the past crap, the darkness of all that. It is difficult, this shedding, apparently, a process. The shifting is hard. There is resistance. Fear. Denial. The releasing of decades of patterning, generations of patterning, whole cultures of patterning. At least forty years of a woman's life, if you don't count the ancestors. "The menstruation era" and all it contained. Changed. I was having trouble shedding this skin on my own, apparently, kept wanting to build on a history of others' expectations, keeping to the norm. I wouldn't have chosen it, necessarily, but now my uterus is scraped clean, a new beginning, fresh, unencumbered. A cleansing and a clearing and now a settling. I just wasn't expecting the need to rest. The lack of energy. The exhaustion. I wasn't expecting it to be a process after the fact. This procedure. Menopause. All of it. I thought I would just be done. Move along with the straight current of energy I was promised. I didn't know I had to make space for the healing. The reforming. Reemerging. I'm new at this, after all.

The predictable narrative arc of storytelling declares just one inciting incident. In the beginning. As women we know they surge again and again and again as we spiral through life and time. There never is just one. There is always something pushing us further into a new emergence. But it takes time. The metamorphosis. The coming out. The never returning, at least not the same way again.

There is another possibility to a story that begins in fear, the threat of death, annihilation.

Where we extract what no longer serves us and reclaim our power, creativity, and autonomy. Where the miniscule falls away from us like rotting flesh and we turn, once again, to our revered role, resurrecting the nurturing relationship of reciprocity we once had with this animate Earth. We are stewards. Caretakers. Co-creators. Not destroyers. Not supplicants.

I picture it like this: We dismantle the dams. Melt the ice. Release. Allow our unbridled creativity to rush into the pulsing of something larger than ourselves, all of it, us, swelling with galloping, passionate currents. We face the flood without fear, a force in our own right, clearing away the debris after the scouring. Then, float in pools of settled calm. Flow easily with joy, happiness, and pleasure. Fluid and flexible grace. We embrace all of it. The whole wild, chaotic, unpredictable, peaceful, beautiful ride on this Earth, in this life. One's own dwelling.

The woman's womb is a portal, a doorway to the dark space beyond, a container, a holding circle of potential. For some women, here enter individual souls meant for individual humans. For me, this has not been the case. Nevertheless, in this silent and dark place, I hold this Void potential, this birthplace of my very own nigredo. A woman's womb is a link to the cosmos, to the divine, to the mystery. No matter how she chooses to use it, it is a creative space. It is sovereignty to create what we choose. Not what others inflict upon us.

For the ancient Celts, the powerful poet class of the Fili were also diviners and seers. They were the link between humans and the Otherworld. Listeners. Translators. Messengers between the land-imbued Sovereignty Goddesses and the people. No chief was without one. I want to fill my belly space with emptiness, a Void into which ideas can flow through, like the sparklings of stars, a comet's tail, clues to the cosmos. I imagine the soul of the world, the soul of this place, entering into my own fruitful darkness, speaking, showing, rising up through my dreams, through my imagination. I pull not children from this space, from this portal place to the beyond, but words.

I gather herbs and flowers from my garden—clusters of white yarrow and the musky citrus of lavender, the purple blooms of oregano, the hardened pod of a poppy—and tie them into a bouquet with twine. I find the winged vertebrae of an elk, long-dried and porous from its days on the forest floor, wrap loose tobacco in a pouch of gold fabric, grab my pen and my journal, and set out with my satchel like a pilgrim for The Lake.

When I arrive, I go immediately to the Grandmother Lodgepole. She is talkative, this tree. Here in this Wasteland, black rock forms multiple undulating hills, cast aside from when the 1920s Pershing Mine extracted 40,000 tons of anthracite coal from this earth. Though ironically made from the crushed bodies of ancient ferns, coal is poor soil for plants. But here is a Lodgepole Pine who has found a way. The Utes call the Lodgepole Ah-gwoop, using her to construct tipis. Settlers used her to make railroad ties in the mining days of the 1800s, pushing the Utes out. For the Celts the pine, Ailm, represented the letter "a" in the Ogham alphabet, first of the vowels. She is known for her hardy tolerance for poor soil. Her root system often runs deep, the tap root extending eleven feet into the ground. Here, growing on the fringe of the waste rock and water, she would have to have these strong suits to create a life.

Her resilient success is apparent.

She rises from a nest of her own fallen and browned needles, several inches deep over the discarded waste rock, gradually decomposing into soil. Scattered about her are piles of her cones, open and relieved of their seeds. A bevy of her children and grandchildren cling to the edges of her skirts. She is doing her part. Healing this place. Making it whole again.

I duck between her arms to her inner sanctum. The cushion of fallen pine needles makes a soft circle directly below the outermost reaches of the branched whorl of her fingertips. Disassembling the piles of rocks cluttered oppressively around her trunk, I move them to the edge of the circle of needles like a hoop, she at the heart. The largest stones I use to mark north, south, east, and west. With a few of the flattest ones I fashion a small altar in a nook of her roots looking east. I place the elk vertebrae on top, tipped on end, and in the hollow where the spinal cord once twitched, insert the bundle of flowers and herbs, along with a stout goose feather I found nearby, as if in a vase. I sprinkle the tobacco about her feet, because I figure this is a language she will recognize, and burn a sprig of sage.

There is a larger flat rock nestled against the trunk of the Grandmother, a perfect sitting stoop, which I do, facing north, the direction of ancestors, home of the wind. Lodgepoles can grow an inch a year in Colorado when in full sun. From her height I guess her childhood began about the time the mine closed, around 100 years ago, when the ground, finally, lay still enough to take root. She is an elder. I lean my back against a century's worth of growth and knowledge, of rain and sun and minerals pulled into woody flesh, listening to the wind in her paired needles, spiraling around each other, as they do, as time does. *Pinus contorta*.

I return the next day to sprinkle the gilded medallions of aspen leaves I cached from one of my favorite fall hikes, to say, "Look, here, what I found. I brought these for you, these pieces of beauty, to share, to offer." Another I bring dried marigolds to place in the four directions, decorating the marking stones. Art as a tool of connection. I pull out my journal and pen. Finally, I think, I am ready.

We live in dark times, deep inside the transformative stuff of the nigredo. From the wonderment, possibility, and obscurity of this liminal space, this uncomfortable squeeze in the initiatory funnel, how shall we emerge? What form will we birth to the burgeoning light?

We have better things to conceive than a pound of flesh extracted according to someone else's toll: a unique and unconventional life, a new way of being ourselves. Resurrecting the parts of our ancient past that serve, an evolving mythology for modern times. An ethic of responsibility and stewardship buried deep in our DNA, rooted in a woman's knowing. We are healers also, after all, now bending our heads and hands to this gaping wound of separation. The needle of truth. Threads of interdependence, inclusion, and balance. Stitching us whole, together, once again. With patience. And repetition.

Creating—

A new story.

And thus—

A new world.

It is a way of seeing as much as anything. A relationship. An interaction. We have all evolved from a single, pulsing source. A divine center. And so a re-membering of the sacred, animate matter of everything. Reuniting with this birthplace. Finished with a mother bear's instinct and ferocity to protect.

"Thank you," I say, bowing deeply, for truly there are no other words.

And then I sit between the kneed roots of the Grandmother Lodgepole. Spine erect along the body of her trunk, looking out to the portal of Womb Water lapping at my toes. Pen poised. Ears pricked.

And I listen.

Song for the black cat outside my mother's apartment

Kinsale Drake

We know what it is to not be wanted,
when our bodies are taboo.

Night limbs, how our eyes
swallow everything

When I was brought into the world,
I looked back.

The trees were heavy with dark.
They say a wicked woman walks

bad luck. What makes a wicked woman?
Irises green with want, barbed tongues

to catch what's coming.
I want to move through the trees

as you do: four palms flush to the earth,
dark river with two wild torches

in a corner: living shadow, the same color
as forgetting.

How many lives
can I hold in each chamber

of my heart?

Feral

Eddi Salado

So long alone I have gone feral
eating rice over the sink

licking blood off a plate
or chewing paper noisily

Four dogs asleep,
nearby a cat

on the counter
grooming herself

and indifferent.
Each with its place.

The hair on my arms
grown lavish.

On my head a witch's mane
or that of a horse

preferring its field
even in winter.

And now you want

to bring me inside
dine at a table

I don't. Know whether
I can drink cream

from a china dish now
Or address silver

orderly as prison bars. Yet
cautiously I fold myself

under your front porch
to wait and wonder

if it is safe
to go inside.

Is it worth the stroke
of your hand on my face,

or the warmth of your lap
to be tamed.

In case you didn't know

Joanne Gram

A bold woman can do a lot of damage

swinging her hips and walking slow

Taking a sloppy sip of coffee

licking up the drips slipping

down the side of a mug or maybe

dragging them off with her lower lip

just so

In case you didn't know or

didn't understand when you took me

by the hand to pull me through the door

I nearly took you by the hand to pull

you with me to the floor

In case you need me to explain

you walking close to me again

ignites a spark that starts

old passions in my brain   in the primal parts

creates that pulse   between my thighs

If I need to clarify my meaning and intentions

paint you a picture in torrid dimensions

I will eat you like a Michigan cherry pie

warmed with whipping cream over the top

take you naughty   take you nicely

simmering sweet   shivering spicy

Just in case you don't recall

our first dance and how we came

to fall into a rolling tide of romance

not always smooth but set up to flow

back to the shore naked as castaways

cast together once more   into more endless days

an island of two in a sea of forgiving

Just in case you already knew

to do these things you always do

gives me reason to hope

we have landed at last

for worse and for better

with our long talking past

pressed into boxes of letters

Come walk with me now

let your hips swing to mine

let my lips nibble the edges

and tips of your tender emotions

as endless we face an endless horizon

where together we move through the

ocean of time

still life (talking)

Stephanie Renée Payne

Mama Johnny's eyes are closed and she's rubbing colored cotton threads between her forefinger and thumb. *Feel'n, baby, just feel'n where they want me to start.* I'm in my five-year-old body again in this old clapboard house. No shoes on my feet, my white leather sandals thrown in the corner, my white cotton shorts and untucked white button-down sleeveless shirt keeping me cool. My mother's way of dressing me. Neat. Clean. *Don't go around looking like a pickaninny*, my mother warns as she kisses me goodbye, her red painted lips barely touching my forehead. She has her rules and her ways. But my mother's gone back to California—back to LA. It's just me and Mama Johnny and Papa Lewis for the entire summer. Free and fanciful on a bright June day. And I'm twirling and dancing in the living room, singing with the radio to the Jackson 5 being my own little *dancing machine* getting as dirty and messy as I please.

Hand me my basket, my grandmother would say. She'd dig through a mess of colored cotton threads and then pick one, or sometimes two, and then she'd go to Jesus—her eyes closed, her head thrown back, her nose pointed toward the heavens. I watched, mesmerized by the spell she was under. Now, in my forty-seven-year-old body, I touch the washed soft fabric of Mama Johnny's quilt that is still pressed and pristine on her bed in her used-to-be room. It's the centerpiece of my grandmother's handwork. *That's mama's pride*, Papa Lewis used to say. *It took Mama twenty Sundays to get that thing done,* he'd tell anyone who admired the quilt with its bleached white edges that Papa said Mama Johnny stubbornly cleaned with a toothbrush. *Mama dun give clean a run for its money.* Papa Lewis told the stories of my grandmother's handwork, pride spilling out of his grin, while Mama Johnny hushed him until he was hushed for good. He passed on—ashes to ashes—a solid twenty years before Mama Johnny's time came. The silence around her handwork, the stories untold after Papa went mute, noticed by everyone. Noticed by me, too, on this day, and in this house with my grandmother's things as my only guide.

Go upstairs! something tells me. As I stand atop the wood pie stairs in the third-floor attic, the voice is even clearer. *Look down!* There's an open window. Its wood frame painted thick coats of slate blue. More paint than wood. *Look down!* Beneath the window is the frozen ground with a sandstone marker as resolute as an Oktibbeha County winter. No more jewel-toned cotton threads dancing between Mama Johnny's fingers. No more stories. No more clues. No more knowing a face that looks like mine. A mirror in a world that doesn't know my existence.

We use'ta bury our people here, Mama Johnny's raspy, cigarette-tinged voice says to me, just as clear as day. And a vision comes to me of my grandmother with her head out that window, blowing circles of smoke from her Marlboros into the Mississippi wind—her secret. Our secret. Papa Lewis never suspected. Mama Johnny keeping that house smelling sweet and clean as she puffed out that window, sucking in that smoke like it was life itself.

With my head out that window, I take a deep breath. Breathing in the Mississippi air, I hear the rocking chair creak, and she appears. A shadow. A ghost, back hunched, eyes bespeckled, bark hands focused on those colored threads. Rocking. Her feet planted on the planked floor that once held up her elegantly tall and slim body. Six feet with no shoes. I want to call out to her, run into the embrace of her open arms. But she might just disappear. I sit myself down in her rocker, and it swallows me. Holds me with its strong oak arms. I slip out of my boots, peel away my wool socks, and let my naked feet rest on the cool wood floor. Pushing myself back and forth. Rocking. I catch a glimpse of how I fit in Mama Johnny's stitching chair. And how I don't. The shadow vision of the woman who loved me—really loved me—slowly fades.

You gonna be better than me, Mama Johnny says on one of my summer visits. *Look at that stitch; it's perfect. Just perfect. Just like you.*

I spot a burlap rag doll in the corner. She's a marvel in white eyelet. She's got this dainty painted-on face—Betty Boop red lips, exaggerated eyelashes, and coal-black eyes. She's tall and proud, and a little sassy, like a stitched-up version of Mama Johnny—a fantasy that maybe my grandmother wanted to be. But then I look closer, and I see the perfect stitching, the precision of the placement of the lace around the hem of her dress, and I can see the part of my grandmother that holds her signature—her way of making something out of nothing with perfection and flair. And here, I feel a settling inside of me, a faint permission to creep toward my own signature—making my own way. A way beyond the downtown law firm where my six-figure graduate school debt landed me, and where I put on a face to match those who have no care for who I am. No need to understand the rumblings of my soul, or how I stand alone and apart—the lone Black woman making them feel charitable in their designer suits and red-bottom shoes, a visitor in the world they so proudly and so ruthlessly created for themselves. But in this house, I can feel my heartbeat again. And even with the distance, three thousand miles from this land with a California sun over my head for most of my life, I know my signature is all wrapped up in hers. The distance evaporates as I rock. I feel myself settling into that chair with the motion, settling into what was never distant to me.

My grandmother's ghost is no longer in the room, but I feel her now inside of me. My ears ringing with her voice, clear and clean. Sister Wind blows a chill through the open window.

Come on, Sister Wind, Mama Johnny'd say on a hot August day out in the dirt, both of us working the land with dribbles of sweat running down our backs. Papa Lewis looming over me on unsteady knees, watching my every move, training me up.

Don't yank at that melon, little bit, twist it. That's right, twist 'til it falls off.

We worked the land just like Mama Johnny's mother, my great-grandma Ginny, and a great-great-grandmother, whose name is unknown, a woman nicknamed "Bunny." Bunny, born a slave, sharecropped the red clay soil in the burning summer sun as a girl. Her hands, as it was told, were even more gnarled than my grandmother's bark-like fingers. But this woman got ownership of the land. The no-named great-great-grandmother was just a fragment in Mama Johnny's memory but a legend in our family. She was a woman who could read and write and had blue eyes, wooly blonde hair, and a mouth that could *cut you to the quick*, Mama Johnny telling me she was part Irish, part slave, part crazy. Her story never fully told.

Remembering, I'm in my little girl body again on a visit, observing, watching, etching into my soul a woman who I didn't know then could be forgotten. I see myself peeking behind doorways, listening in the dark, always trying to catch the magic that Mama Johnny held. Imagining, I let myself know my grandmother as a girl. I see her skinny and long running in the grass, running through this old house in the declining Black side of Starkville, Mississippi. I let myself hear Mama Johnny's little girl voice practice the spelling of her state's name in her schoolhouse: *Miss-little i-ss-little i-pp-little-i.* And here, I understand that it takes more courage than I could have ever known on that plane from Los Angeles to embrace the joys and sorrows and truths of a woman who created magic with her hands. And here, I want to root where I belong. Root inside the land that kindled Mama Johnny and Mama Ginny and all the mamas before them, women who loved me when I was just the seed of a promise. With their heads tilted to the sky and their noses pointed to the heavens, and their eyes closed tight, those women made magic with whatever the land gave them, and with hands as strong as the trees that line the hard-won property that I now stand on. They knew me and they knew themselves.

And maybe that knowing *is the magic*. And maybe it's the way Mama Johnny, my mother's mother, made everything make sense. She took the deaths of the two out of the six children she birthed as a fact of living in this life and in her skin. She took Papa Lewis's *crazy war mind* that the VA could never or would never solve as fate, and the care of her husband as her proud duty. My grandmother was sturdy and sullen and joyful and her cussing like lyrics to a song: *Mother-fucking-cotton-picking-narrow-yellow-ass heifer*. She had a rhythm to her. It was in her body, in the way her long arms swung when she walked, in the way she cocked her head to the side when she knew I was fibbing or about to cry *for no good goddam reason*. Mama Johnny never shed a tear that I could see. But I knew she felt pain. She'd moan and rock in her stitching chair. She'd stitch and iron seams and push her glasses up on the bridge of her nose to inspect her work. And no matter what was happening inside her body or mind, and no matter who was present or what time of day, when she saw me, her eyes lit up, and her long arms reached for me and held my dirt-smudged, little dancing self in a way that I now know is rare and sweet and fleeting.

In this room, in her chair, and in this cold and empty house, I can hear her tearless moans slipping from her stitching chair. I hear mine, too, as I rock. As we rock. And I know, I just know that Mama Johnny's history is tangled with mine, and that I can hold her, too. And here, something forms inside of me that wasn't there before—why I was called to this place.

Why? my mother asked when I told her I wanted to stay in Mississippi. *There's nothing for you there. You'll throw away all your hard work living in a place like that.* My mother, Shirl, was Mama Johnny's only daughter. Shirl got on a bus at nineteen and shimmied her pretty, red-bone, good-hair self into the promised city of Los Angeles to pursue the life she dreamed of—a rich husband, a fancy house, a lost southern accent. But she, too, moans when tears have no place to root. My mother is a part of the land just like her mother, and her mother's mother, and unnamed, unknown, and unremembered mothers—our legacy. Just like all our stolen people with our stolen histories and stolen tears. But those tears are alive in the soil and water, and in my grandmother's body that is now settled in the ground beneath the third-floor attic window—a little stone marker testifying that she was here. Dust to dust. The land holds the memory that Mama Johnny spent her whole life trying to forget. She had an efficient and clever way of forgetting. She'd clutch those colored cotton threads between her fingers and focus on what those threads wanted to say on clean white cloth. *Just feel'n, baby*. She felt her way through her pain. She rocked herself clear and clean until the window called her name and beckoned her back to the land.

While Your Back Was Turned

Hampton Williams Hofer

The boys let the screen door slam. They spun out into the grass, all noise and skin, Brunswick stew in their bellies, Cassius Clay in their minds. Nora sat on the sofa in the lamplight in her pink socks and her mother's lumpy knit sweater waiting for Ed Sullivan. The show would start in ten minutes, *Live from Miami Beach*, but the boys could not sit waiting for ten minutes. She would call them back in during the Lipton Tea commercial and they'd come trampling, cold hands, hot breath. In the kitchen, her parents sat back down at the green linoleum table that had been wiped clean of stray lima beans, their heads close together.

"They said they won't have any space until she's in her seventh month," said Nora's father. He had driven thirty minutes round-trip to his office to make the phone call, because it was Sunday and no one would be there.

"Well, everyone will know by then, Peter," said Nora's mother, one foot tucked beneath her like a child on the chair. "Will you have some more water? Your face is red."

"I'm alright," he said. "Maybe you could call the Donnellys. See if they can pull some strings at the place in DC."

"I can't do that, Peter. It would be as good as front-page news the next day."

"And the doctor?" Nora's father touched his hair. "You're sure? Maybe I should call him myself."

"It's too late for all of that," said Nora's mother. "Open the door, will you? It's too stuffy. That's why you're all flushed." Nora's father got up and opened the kitchen door, allowing the boys' grunts and cheers to filter in with the February night. In six years, the lottery would call them, one by one, onto the ships to the Far East, and in their swaying bunks at night they would ache to press their cheeks to the backyard grass again.

"So it's down to your sister's then," said Nora's father. "Just for the summer."

Nora's mother lowered her chin and looked up at him. "It'll have to be earlier. Look at her sweater, Peter. Maybe another month at most."

"Easter then," said Nora's father.

"Easter," said her mother, getting up to fill a glass at the sink and bringing it over. "You really are so red." In the living room, Nora cranked up the volume and they could hear Ed Sullivan's voice.

"It's on!" Nora yelled.

"What is that accent he's got?" asked Nora's mother.

"Boston, I think," said Nora's father.

"I think it's New York."

"What difference does it make?"

Nora hollered for the boys again, and they all packed the sofa. No time wasted on the introduction, the opening chords, and then the curtain lifted.

She loves you yeah, yeah, yeah. The screen prickled. Nora and the boys all smiled with open mouths, ticking shoulders and bobbing feet, moving despite themselves. Nora's parents stood behind the sofa to watch, as if sitting somewhere would indicate approval.

"And what about at the end of the summer?" asked Nora's father, arms crossed over his chest, eyes on the four suited figures on the screen.

"Well, then she'll come home," said Nora's mother. "We're lucky on the timing, don't you see? With it being summer and all." *She loves you yeah, yeah, yeah.*

"So she'll come home," said Nora's father. "Just her."

"Of course just her, Peter," said Nora's mother. "We really are so very lucky on the timing."

Nora's aunt's burnt-orange bungalow in Tallahassee was only a ten-minute walk from the university, its dives and shops, the farmers' market, the hospital where she would go. Nora's aunt gave her a gold band to wear on her left hand when they went out. Where Nora had grown slowly at first, she now burgeoned like bread dough in the heat, dipping over the sides of everything, a hand on her lower back when she moved. The days were the same. She ate oatmeal crème pies and drank grape Fanta, flipping through *TeenSet* magazine in the white plastic lounge chair beneath the live oak in the side yard and listening to the British Invasion on the radio. Sometimes at the dinner table, Nora's aunt would see the way Nora's stomach moved with the rolling on the inside. Nora's aunt was younger than her mother, but gray, her face a finely wrinkled map of sun and smoke and adventures untold.

"Do you want to feel it?" Nora asked. They were on the screen porch, mopping up shrimp and crab casserole with slabs of cornbread.

"Oh, I really don't think I ought to," said Nora's aunt. Nora thought she understood why.

"I could stay here with you," Nora said. "We could."

"Your parents wouldn't have that, and you know it," said Nora's aunt.

"What'll they do?" said Nora. "Come and lift me up like a child? Drag me to the car and make me leave?"

"We'd better not find out," said Nora's aunt.

"I'll be eighteen in two months," Nora said.

"It really wouldn't make any difference." Nora's aunt pinched a shrimp where the body met the tail and pulled it cleanly out with her teeth. She had never grown the way Nora grew now, had never seesawed between the earthly and the divine that way. "What did he look like?" she asked.

"Better than melted butter," Nora said, and her aunt hummed. The truth was that his face was already a painting left out in the rain. Now he was only a red baseball jersey in the outfield, the back of an amber head a few pews in front, the glow of a white T-shirt in the dark of the backyard where he waited for her to climb down, arms open if she missed a hitch in the trellis. He was red and amber and white—heat and light.

"Does he know any of this?" her aunt asked.

Nora shook her head. "He wouldn't, would he?"

"No," she said. "I supposed he wouldn't."

It was like that for the hot and lonely summer when it was just Nora and her aunt and the one inside who kicked to be known but who could not be hers.

It was a late afternoon, the sun setting the orange bungalow ablaze, when the pains started, when they washed Nora into a place she had never been, and through the water she could hear her aunt's voice: "Here comes the needle. Just a little shot. It'll all be right over. All over in a jiff."

Nora awakes and it is over. Her aunt is next to the bed.

"There you are," says Nora's aunt. "I just hung up from your mother. She and your daddy will be on their way down tomorrow or the day after."

Nora says nothing. Her aunt pats her hand.

"It's all done, honey. You're all done," says her aunt. "Did you hear? Your mother and daddy are coming soon to get you. They'll take you back home now."

"Home?" Nora says.

"You know school starts Monday after next," says Nora's aunt. "Aren't you excited for your senior year? Cap and gown and all that?"

"Gown?" says Nora.

"You know all the graduation hoopla. All the fun senior stuff. That'll start Monday after next. You already look so much more like yourself," says her aunt.

Nora notices for the first time the white sheets of the narrow bed, the early gray light through the window, the pale yellow phone on the wall.

"What did I have?" she says.

"I'm not sure."

"Sure you are."

"Oh, darling, they said it would be best truly if you just didn't know," says Nora's aunt.

"Well, why would that be?"

"It's for the best that way, really. It is. They say it's always done that way."

"But *you* know."

"I really can't be sure," says Nora's aunt.

Later, when the window is black, Nora stands. Her hair is still damp from the shower, her feet cold on the tiled floor. Her stomach tightens and she feels a gush that wets her padded underpants. She squints in the fluorescent light of the bathroom and cleans herself, pressing a hand to her soft, empty middle. She cannot find socks, so shoves into her sneakers instead.

She walks down the hall to the windowed room. Bassinets in three rows, most empty.

Even through the glass, she knows which one. She knows it the same way she knows that she is hungry, that it is nearly morning. She knows it the way she knows that she is alive.

A nurse is staring at Nora as she walks into the room, as she moves to the bassinet and peers down at the face that the rain had blurred. She lifts the tight package up to her chest.

"It ain't right what they did." The voice startles her, and she grips the package tighter. It makes a noise like an animal.

"Didn't mean to scare you," says the nurse in her white apron and cap. "I let you come in and touch, but you gotta go before someone fires me for it."

"What is it?" Nora asks.

"It's a girl," says the nurse.

"I knew," says Nora.

"But you really gotta—" the nurse starts.

"I named her Lillian Elena because saying it makes my tongue do a tap dance like Shirley Temple," Nora says.

"Please now," says the nurse.

"Do you think it's a pretty name?"

"It's a real pretty name. It is. But you're gonna get us in trouble," says the nurse.

"What if you turned around to go tend to that one?" says Nora, nodding to the wriggling cocoon fussing in the bassinet at the end of the row. "And then if you did, you wouldn't have any idea about what happened while your back was turned." Nora still holds the package to her chest, bobbing up and down on the balls of her feet.

"Oh, honey," says the nurse. "You won't get far. I wish you would. I really do. But you won't get far." The cocoon on the end is getting louder, threatening to wake the others.

"That's okay," says Nora, thinking maybe the nurse is right and maybe she is wrong. And then the nurse turns around and leans over, busy changing the screamer's diaper.

It is black in the hall and through the windows. The closed doors, the empty desk. The parking lot is a sea of black. Nora is wet again, in her underpants and at her chest. She is a shadow on the sidewalk. But it feels good to move and the night is warm, and she holds tight as she heads toward the streets she knows, toward the burnt-orange bungalow. A car passes slowly but doesn't stop, tunes through the open windows. *She loves you yeah yeah yeah.*

I'm Not the Heroine of Your Cancer Novel

Laura E. Garrard

I won't star in your afterschool special,
You expect me to fill your courage bill,
Want the gory chemo details,
The rancid toilet, the clichés?
Not every patient pukes after treatment
Nor loses their hair, and one who has, says to me
Thank God, you don't need to share such stories,
If you did, I would puke again from the mere mention.
He doesn't wear these passage rites as banners.

You trigger my trauma,
Mind and body flooded so
I can't talk, only tremble,
Don't think clearly for hours
After you challenge me in class,
Write this poem as if speaking to Cancer.
You don't hold the right to decide
Where and when I should overcome
Because you think me strong.
I need strength to soothe more important shocks.

Though how can you know this is wrong,
Our culture wants cancer heroes, survivors
Of these diseases beyond our control.
I don't take it personally, really, but my body does.

Cancer realities are not dramas
To raise up as martyrs.
These words are not meant to inspire leaders,
They seek to resonate, embalm little wisdoms
That seep from beyond the grave,
Share hard-earned humility and advocacy,
Admit honest low moments, proffer hope.
Many patients and docs will tell you
Cancer paths walk largely in the head and heart—
Stress over diagnoses, and yes treatments,
Fear about death.

If you want more bile in your book,
Volunteer on an infusion wing of
Traditional hard-hitting *chemotherapy*.
Thankfully, I've not piped it into
My petite, hard-to-poke veins
Because I know this body won't take it.
I stop *immunotherapy* infusions as soon as
Veins object by turning red afterward,
And I show a safe level of improvement.
Complete remission isn't always achieved,
Instead I follow this body's needs and signals
As gently as able, live faithful to instinct,
Support my most successful survival,
Keep what's working of my own immune system
As long as possible.

One doctor says he cures myeloma, (30–40% chance of)
Suggests I start with traditional chemo—
The possible effects, including death,
Blur my vision just reading about them—
Then three rounds of four drugs, a double,
Meaning dying twice, bone marrow transplant
That first kills your entire blood system,
Replaced by stem cell reintroduction
While at risk of fatal infection,
Followed by three years of the initial four drugs.
He says, You're young, you'll do well—No, I just can't do it,
Know I'll die from these treatments.
Decide to rely on scientific research,
Control disease by least intervention
Needed to sustain quality-lived life.
New drugs are on the rise.

I'm not in a battle with cancer,
I'm enduring to heal my mind-body,
So don't misappropriate my story,
If it's macabre and victory you want,
Read a war novel.
I may never win your cancer-free ribbon,
Yet my pages still turn.

If the Word for You Is Dyke

Robin Percyz

I've got a folder in my camera roll called "Dyke Roots."
Created as a tongue-in-cheek joke for "what made me queer"
is now a technicolor manifesto of "what saved my life."

It's chock full o' "DYKONS," dyke-adjacent people, and pop culture artifacts
with cues on how to love, who to love,
and how to "wear dyke" like a bad bitch with style.

Never underestimate the power of visibility,
even if it was invisible to you as a six-year-old.
Do estimate the years added to your life

because a Black, butch guitarist named Me'Shell Ndegeocello
rocked your world harder
than John Mellencamp in the "Wild Night" music video.

Do thank 90s NYC for blessing you with RENT on Broadway,
a queer rainbow of otherness having an orgy
teaching you that love wins, decades before "love wins."

Oh yeah, and that sex can look and feel different
than your Ken and Barbie missionary tales of yore.
Measure your life in love.

Measure it in how many years you've been sober
because you fell in love with P!NK at 15
and she's still saving your 38-year-old life.

Do bow down on your knees to the Black trans women before you.
Bow down to Marsha P. Johnson and the Stonewall Riots
for laying the bloody red carpet of freedom that you skip on.

I believe in the unconscious knowing of queerness.
That we navigate the streets and look up just as a fellow queer is
    within our gaze.
Gays!

It's not happenstance, it's magic, because we are. Like a superpower.
When we lock eyes, squint, and do the gay nod that
silently screams "we see each other,"

laser beams bind us together in a cotton candy universe
straight out of a Lisa Frank animation,
where we are saddled on unicorns, flying through clouds of rainbows,

landing gingerly on a golden, glitter-flecked brick road
staring head on into the eyes of another queer.
You are safe here. You are home.

It sounds fantastical and mythical
because that is what queer acceptance is after being locked in a
    chamber of shame,
muzzled, gagged, and drowned by alcohol.

I don't hide anymore. I don't limit myself to the either/or,
the femme/butch binary of "lipstick lesbian" or "diesel dyke."
We're a world within a world on the dyke spectrum. You can have it
    all, be it all.

I scream "femme dyke"
from the bottom of my cunt
to the tip of my boxing glove.

Get you a dyke who can do both:
beat her face with red rouge,
then beat another's with a nasty right hook.

If the word for you is "dyke,"
wear it like a bare chest without a bra.

Wear it like a first-choice word: don't say "lesbian"
to make them comfortable if that's not what feels right to you.

Wear it like your high heels or Doc Martens
are stomping the patriarchy with every saunter.

Wear it in a skin tight mini dress, a three-piece suit, a tight lineup
on your butch, masculine-of-center head, or anything in between.

Wear it like a woman, trans woman, or non-binary
HUMAN who rejects TERFs.

Wear it like a pussy riot against governments that want to erase
your love, your rights, your identity.

Wear it like an Alcoholics Anonymous chip
after 17 years of sobriety, a badge of honor.

If the word for you is dyke, stop what you're doing,
and create a folder in your camera roll labeled "Dyke Roots."

Laugh. Then cry as you add artifacts of people and things that saved
   your life.
Laugh that cis-het people don't require the privilege

of a folder on their phone dedicated to being a superhero.
Beating death over and over throughout life.

I don't believe in religion, but I believe in dykes.
And if there is a God, she's a Black, butch Goddess who saved my life.

If the word for you is dyke, I fucking love you.
I love us.

Monkey Balls

Connie Corzilius

The Yard Man's stubby fingers stroked and stroked his goatee, which fell lank and underachieving to the stretched-out collar of his sweat-soaked T-shirt. Celebrating a downtown bar, the T-shirt was no doubt acquired in his drinking days, which weren't far behind him (*a year sober*, he had offered). Middle-aged? Younger? He was muscled, but he'd seen hard miles.

I don't leave Summertown, he continued, referring to their neighborhood, which was old and green and Southern in a way only outsiders recognized. *I limit my business to a few customers so I can focus you get what I'm saying? I'm a detail guy.*

His mirrored sunglasses threw her own distorted face back at her, and he carried some sort of gnarled stick as he strode around the yard, poking things with it or suddenly squatting to finger leaves and stems. "Oh, okay," Jane thought, "an eccentric."

And because she too was a bit of an oddball (at sixty-five, may as well admit it); and because she thought of herself as someone who appreciated eccentrics (hadn't she been an art major once upon a time?); and because she had a certain idea of herself as laid-back (in short, as "cool")—she gave him the job.

From the beginning, she never knew which yard man would show up. Some days, he buzzed. He fizzed. He had plans for her yard, big plans.

You'll never believe this cool thing super cool thing but I passed this house old house old lady one of the OG gardeners you get what I'm sayin'? Had every kind of Southern plant and flower but she died and they sold it to some young couple don't know shit ripping out plants left and right and I said hey mind if I take some? They didn't care didn't know what they got just stupid yuppies so I loaded up. I don't got a clue what all's in here but figure I'll just plant 'em and we'll see what comes up kind of a grab bag thing you dig?

"Um, sure, okay." Though he hadn't asked her permission.

She retreated to the house and watched him through the blinds. If Arthur were still alive, they would have spied on him together, dissecting his behavior and speculating about his life. Arthur, who lacked patience, had been apt to consign people to the wastebin for their oddities. "Jesus, what a chucklehead," he might have said, and thus, another nickname would have been born. They'd assigned secret names, many unflattering, to most of the neighbors on their walking route. Something small, but it yoked them together, and she missed it.

"What's Chuckles doing now?" Arthur whispered, and she smiled. They'd been married almost forty years; it was easy to imagine their conversation.

She watched as the Yard Man came to a complete, motionless stop, as if contemplating Nature in all its fecund glory. Then he jerked back to awareness and took up a new task, leaving the old one undone.

"Jesus," Arthur said.

Other times, the Yard Man was withdrawn, surly. His words were context-free, as if he'd been having a conversation in his head and had only begun verbalizing it when she approached.

I went to college you know and still everyone looks down on me I see them drive by real slow they're keeping an eye on me you think I'm KIDDING? The big lawncare guys I'm encroaching on their territory they see me. They see me. Like I'm not qualified I went to college what do they got? All the work THAT'S what . . . yeah they got all the work like I don't deserve my slice . . . like I don't work fuckin' twelve-hour days for peanuts. They see me.

This was not what Jane had hoped for, which was what— smooth dealings? A laugh or two, the warmth of fellow feeling? She wasn't sure, but his comings and goings ruched the fabric of her day, jangled her nerves, and the *peanuts* part hadn't escaped her, either. O, unjust! She had asked and he had provided a figure, to which she had agreed. He had set his own price!

"Listen, if you feel I'm not paying you enough, we can talk about it. Maybe now you're doing the work, you think it's not adequate after all, and that's fine, really. What *do* you think is fair?"

She stood on the driveway, squinting in the bright sunlight, wearing Arthur's oversized T-shirt and the old lady crops that spared the world the sight of her scarred knees, her gray hair—uncut since Arthur died—fading into the backdrop of cement. He did not look up.

"So, what do you think?" she asked again, more forcefully.

He shook his head. *Idiots. Gonna move this lantana, never should of been planted here in the first place.* Then he rose from his squat, turned, and walked to his truck.

"Hey!" she wanted to shout. "I'm standing right here!"

She thought he was going to grab his shovel, but instead he climbed in his old brown truck, jammed it into gear, and drove off.

Arthur had been gone for nearly a year, yet she felt his presence in the house. Maybe that's why she preferred to putter around at home, one ear alert to the eddies and currents, catching stray phrases as they drifted by. Miraculously, she'd discovered she could have her medications and groceries delivered, and she couldn't remember the last time she'd gotten gas for her Subaru, which gathered pine pollen in the carport. It hadn't always been that way, of course. Not that they'd ever been "joiners," not really, but she and Arthur had had their pursuits. Hikes with the local Audubon chapter. Shifts at the food bank. The occasional lecture at the Unitarian Church. A quiet life, but a rich one.

"I don't like this Chuckles fellow," Arthur said now. "He's a loser."

"Oh, come on, Arthur. Not everyone has a PhD." Arthur had been a professor of botany, but like stylists with fried hair or physicians who smoked, he could not muster interest in their lawn and so was apt to purchase the most mainstream cultivar at the big box store just to get it over with. "Habitat, not horticulture, Jane, habitat not horticulture!" he had exclaimed more times than she could count. And so the yard was hers, except for a small patch in the northwest corner where he experimented with odd plants in his tinkering, academic fashion. The plot was his bailiwick; she knew not to mess with it, and she had warned the Yard Man to steer clear.

"Maybe cut Chuckles some slack," she said to Arthur now. "He's in recovery."

"'In recovery'? Is that what they call it now?" Sometimes she couldn't remember if it was Arthur or she who had spoken.

She knew her friends—acquaintances, really—thought she had withdrawn from the world, but the way she saw it, the world had withdrawn from *her*. It seemed all her specificity had worn off, been rubbed off by use and time, and she had become something featureless and smooth their eyes slid past. Her color had dimmed, her hair paled, her eyes competed with the sun damage on her face, mere knotholes in a speckled tree.

Her face in the mirror both angered and frightened her.

Maybe she still clung to Arthur because he was the last person who had actually seen her.

She never knew when the Yard Man might show up, which offended her sense of order, and he often left jobs half-finished. Still, they managed to get through the summer.

The real problems started with the sweet gum balls.

I hate coming here. He accosted her one day in early fall as she was on the way to the mailbox. *Hate dealing with these goddamn monkey balls.*

"Excuse me, monkey balls?"

He nudged a sweet gum ball with the toe of his boot, then kicked it her way.

"Oh. I know they're a pain, but it's not like it's a surprise. You knew that we had sweet gum trees when I hired you."

Again, she offered to pay him more, and again he ignored her, revving up the blower and turning away. She felt like a fool, invisible on her own property.

Now, she spied on him every time he came, going from window to window, watching through a chink in the blinds. She read anger in his gait, the way he treated his equipment; she saw his lips move and knew he was venting to himself. Sometimes he paced the yard to no obvious end. Sometimes he came and then left after fifteen minutes. Sometimes he sat in his truck, motor running, for half an hour.

"I don't like it, Jane." She could feel Arthur hovering near her shoulder. "The guy's paranoid." She ignored him, moving to the bedroom window to get a better look.

Once, in a bout of nostalgia, she had ordered some patchouli incense online, a woo-woo-looking shop with effusive reviews. Inside the package was a second tissue-paper packet tied with purple string and tagged with a handwritten note: *Enjoy the lagniappe!* A label (*To protect you and yours*) was affixed to the small plastic bag, and nestled inside were three sweet gum balls.

She had laughed till her stomach hurt. Coals to Newcastle! (Did anyone even know what that meant anymore?) Outside, the sweet gum balls fell and fell and fell some more, massing, building, threatening her passage across the grass, from sidewalk to driveway, and driveway to mailbox.

He wasn't even trying to keep up.

Hey! he yelled, pounding on the front door. *Hey!* until the plaster shook. He'd never done that before, and it rattled her.

"What's wrong?" she asked when she got outside.

Fuck, he said. *FUCK. I just spent an HOUR a solid HOUR blowing these fucking monkey balls. I had no idea that in this yard in THIS yard the monkey balls are the only thing that matter. Like legit the ONLY THING. Get rid of the monkey balls whatever you do!* he said in a falsetto voice. Then: *Fuck. FUCK FUCK FUCK.*

She took a step back. How had she let it come to this?

I mean I HAD NO IDEA, he said, practically growling.

"They're not *the* thing, they're *a* thing," she said, prim even to her own ears.

I do the work people think they're too good to do. They think it's beneath them. He was muttering, and she wasn't sure if he was talking to her or to himself.

"It's never been a problem for anyone else," she said before she could stop herself.

Maybe you should ask THEM to do it then. You know I don't have to do this I can make a lot more money foraging mushrooms. You don't even know. I'm like a my—a MYCOLOGIST man! Go into the woods with my sack and come out with those babies man you can't believe what I can charge. I know the poison from the payday I just do this on the side. Make a lot more doin' that. You don't even know.

He was so full of shit.

"Nothing's stopping you," she wanted to say. Instead, she handed him his check, which he snatched with grubby hands, though he still hadn't cashed the last one.

She was shaken all that week. A car would backfire or a neighbor would crank up a power tool and she'd rush to the window, sure that he'd returned. After a few days, she moved to the porch, hoping to get a better view of his arrival, but he did not come that week or the next.

"This is pathetic," she thought, "sitting on the porch like a goddamn John Prine song." The leaves piled up and the sweet gum balls fell and she texted him, finally: "Are you coming back or what?"

He showed up at 7 a.m. the next morning, though the ordinance prohibited operating machinery until 8 a.m., and between his whistling and his blowing he made a horrible racket. When he left, she charged out to the yard, quite sure that he'd blown the sweet gum balls under the hedges and shrubs rather than taking them away like he was supposed to, and she was so angry to find that she was right that she kicked at a cluster of toadstools that had sprung up—saw their pale, tentacular undercarriage—right before she rolled her foot on a sweet gum ball, lost her balance, and fell on her ass, her ankle hot and swelling.

She sat there, near crying, as much from anger as from pain, and while she caught her breath, she looked at the sweet gum balls on the ground around her, really *looked* at them. Arthur had wanted to take the trees down, but she loved their fall color and had made a case for keeping them. "Those spiny brown balls are actually the *fruit* of the tree, Arthur," she'd said, reading from Wikipedia. "The balls are made up of capsules, and each capsule contains several small seeds—isn't that cool?" Ludicrous, in retrospect, reading Wikipedia to a botanist, but he'd relented, lacking patience for what amounted to a meaningless fight.

She didn't have her phone and there was no one to call anyway, so she struggled to get up, wincing when she tried to put weight on her foot. The thought of urgent care made her feel ill. Those people. Looking right through her. Calling her *dear*. Didn't she have Arthur's cane somewhere, the one he'd used toward the end—in the carport storage, maybe?

It was slow going, but she limped to the carport, found the cane amid the boxes and bags she'd not yet marshalled the strength to sort, and rested for a moment, her gaze soft, unfocused, a feeling stealing over her, something not quite right. The backyard was as clear as the front yard was ratty. But more than clear, it was empty, the sun not so much illuminating as interrogating every square foot.

And then she saw it: Arthur's plot, every plant taken down to the mulch, now nothing but stubble, the wreckage already browning in the Georgia sun. She doubled over, the slaughter a sock in the gut, the cane the only thing that kept her from dropping to her knees.

Petals—delicate, velvety—lay curling, brutally uncoupled from their green brethren, and the stalks and stems lay broken, most cut, but some merely bent in half, creased and suffering, as if assaulted by hand. As if a man, a small man, a pissy man, had thrown a tantrum and turned on their pale beauty, bent on destruction.

She could feel their pain, hear their keening in the face of this betrayal. For what else could it be, but betrayal?

Arthur's garden. Arthur's.

He was gone and it was her responsibility to seek recompense, though there was no recompense. There was only waiting for another season, another turn around the sun, another pile of long, dull days.

Except. Except.

"Please come by tomorrow," she texted him. "We need to talk."

When Arthur had first died, she felt as if she'd gone underground to join him, the days ahead like a tunnel that looked impossibly narrow till it reached utter convergence, a vanishing point. She knew it was all in the perspective, that when you got there the path would be just as wide, and passable, and possible. That's what they'd said, and she'd believed them—all the friends she no longer heard from. All the self-help books she'd dumped in Little Libraries all over town. She had believed them until the walls did indeed close in and she found herself at a dead stop at that utter convergence, that vanishing point. Not a trick of perspective after all.

The Yard Man was clearly put out when he arrived, his lower lip jutting and his hands clinched, as if ready to mix it up. They did not greet each other; instead, she led him (and if he noticed that her ankle was wrapped and she was using a cane, he did not let on) around back and to the far corner, where he had laid waste.

How do you like it? he said, before she could get a word out. Jaunty. Defiant.

"I have been nothing but nice to you," she began. He just stood there, petting his greasy goatee. He was not going to make this easy, but that was hardly a surprise. She took a deep breath. "Look, why did you do this? I told you to leave this corner alone. I was very clear about it."

He stretched, first one arm, then the other, all browned limbs and pit stains, the epitome of indifference.

"Well?"

I guess I'm surprised you're not happy. You said you wanted the monkey balls cleared all eleven-million of 'em so I thought I'd clear it all clear everything give you a nice clean empty yard. I know you don't like anything . . . messy. He smirked.

"The thing is, those plants were valuable, at least to me. They're entheogens."

Entheogens. Okay. And?

"And? Do you even know what those are, entheogens? They're psychoactive plants, consciousness altering. My husband was a botanist, remember? I told you?"

So like what—?

"He had a special interest in them, academic and otherwise. He did experiments, you know, like with different growing conditions, to see how they affected the concentrations of psychoactive compounds, and then—" She paused. "And then, he harvested them to make tea."

Tea?

"Yes, tea, and I was going to do the same this year, my first harvest alone, but now I can't."

Huh. Wow.

"Right, *wow,*" she almost spat. "You ripped them out of the ground, my husband's plants, destroyed them, and for what? To prove some point?"

You're telling me they get you high? Like, for real? He seemed, almost, to be paying attention to her.

"Yes, for real."

Shit. Well can't you use them anyway? Harvest them? To make tea I mean. He dropped to his knees and swept the uprooted brown and wilted green with both arms, making a pile.

"I don't know. I don't know, maybe, but there's no point now. I can't stand to look at them like that, it depresses me. Just clean them up and get them out of here, will you?"

She and Arthur watched from the window as he went to his truck and got his knapsack.

"There goes Chuckles," Arthur said. "Living up to our worst expectations. Are you sure this is the way to go, Jane?"

"I'm sure."

She hated firing people, and who knows if he would even hear her? If it would even register?

But she would not have to fire him after all.

Together, they watched him gather the drying plants, leaves and stems, roots and petals, and place them in his knapsack. As gentle now as he was brutal before.

Getting high was never their thing. A glass of wine before dinner maybe, but nothing more mind-altering than that. No, Arthur's garden had been a pet project, the side venture of an enthusiast. He'd published papers about it. She remembered the last one, released just a few weeks before he died. "Neurotoxins in Common

Plants: Water Hemlock Poisoning Presenting as Convulsive Status Epilepticus."

Nothing as prosaic as sweet gum balls for him, or cheap highs, either. No, he preferred Belladonna. Water hemlock. White snakeroot. So fascinating, so poisonous. The little patch of vegetation she'd warned Chuckles away from had been Arthur's hobby and haven, nothing but glorious phytotoxins. The Yard Man would know that if he knew all he claimed to know, but he was just a yard man after all.

And now she'd have to find another one.

She watched as he drove away, her reflection in the window surprisingly distinct, not spectral at all. She was prickly and complicated, goddamn it. There were seeds, still, in those spines.

Queen of Wands

Stephanie Whetstone

Annie had spent the whole morning trying to pack, but it wasn't going well. There were too many clothes spread all over the bed. They would never fit into the small backpack she was determined to take, and she couldn't decide what she'd really need. Do you really need anything? She was falling into existential questions. That's what happened when you really didn't want to go somewhere, but insisted out loud that you did. When the anxiety thumping in your chest and neck held you hostage. Forward was always the hardest direction.

Annie had stopped listening to what her heart told her. It had led her astray so many times, who could believe it now? She had signed up for this though, said she wanted it, and now her bed was strewn with clothes for every potentiality: rain, heat, sleet, snow, she didn't know what to do for hail. Stay inside, maybe? That she could do. She was not a camper. Not a happy one at least, but this would be a cabin, far away from everything. Far the fuck away. That was the one thing Annie knew she wanted.

In real life, she had to talk to her ex every day, for one reason or another. So much is intertwined when you've been married for nearly thirty years. Important things have been assigned to one brain or the other. But you would not believe how much each conversation weighed. More than she did; more than he did. "A fucking lot, Marco!" she told him. That sentence alone weighed fifty pounds. Annie was ready for pretend life, idyllic life, and that is what the website promised.

Her kids came home every few weeks now, to do laundry and eat all they could scavenge. "Where's the milk?" Oscar asked, peering deeply into the fridge, willing a gallon to appear.

"I don't buy it anymore. I'm lactose intolerant, always have been." He didn't acknowledge what she said, just put his headphones back on and left the kitchen.

"We need milk," Kate said, looking at the empty shelves for guidance. None came. The kids didn't consider Annie's body, her intolerances. They wanted what they wanted, and since the day they were born, Annie had gotten it for them.

They were good company though, mostly, asked if she was okay, hugged her tight. But they added more weight, grown as they were. And who knew if anybody was okay? Weren't most people always on the brink of tears, ready to weep at any moment? Or was that just her?

Sometimes, Annie's friends stopped by "just to check in." You get the picture. Weight. More mouths to feed, dishes to clean once they were gone. Annie was waiting for her head to still on the inside. It had been spinning for months. She couldn't focus enough to watch a whole movie, let alone read a book. Thank God her book club was all about the wine. She focused on the things she had always focused on—the bills, the laundry, groceries—but now that she wasn't managing logistics for four people, she had the strange sensation that something else was filling her life: time. What the hell do you do with that? Like, how do you choose something to do, rather than let the business of middle management carry you through the days? Hello, time, Annie said, pulling a chair out for it. Sit down. I think we need to talk.

The brochure came in the mail: imagine that—something in the mailbox that wasn't a bill or a Bed Bath & Beyond coupon! Annie had almost accidentally thrown it away with all the other junk mail, but she caught a glimpse of the photo of the fire pit in front of the small cabin and rescued it from the trash. Flame. That was what she needed. To be alone in a cabin in the woods with a fire at this point seemed exotic and somehow absolutely necessary. She fantasized about "burning it all to the ground," as her friend Shelly always said. Metaphorically of course, but the fire looked powerful. Annie wanted powerful.

"Why don't you just come to my place for a few days?" Shelly said. "We could get some wine, watch movies—read tarot cards! I've been practicing." Shelly always assigned Annie the Page of Swords and herself the Queen of Cups. No offense, Shelly, but Annie didn't want to be a page. She wanted to be queen. Somebody's queen. Anybody's queen. The queen of Annieland. Yaas, Queen. Annie wanted a piece of that. This cabin could be the capitol of Annieland, the county seat. She made a random pile of the clothes on the bed and packed them, threw her suitcase in the back of the car, cued up her audiobook, and drove west.

Annie pulled the wagon into the gravel drive of the cabin, crunching to a stop. It had taken her longer than she'd expected to get here—the wrong turn around Philly had added an hour—so the light was fading now, the sky quickly darkening in the shadows of the tall pines. This was Virginia, the Blue Ridge, but this late, it was the black ridge. The sky was pocked with silver stars. Annie stepped out of the car and looked out—wow. A blanket of stars. People said that, in poems and novels about love, but wow. Damn. It was a fucking blanket. Annie wanted to wrap herself in it. If the stars stayed in the same place, no matter how far you drove, why were they a blanket here and only a couple of stitches in New York? Why was her life unraveling?

The small wood cabin consisted of two big rooms: a kitchen/living/dining room and a bedroom, with a tiny bathroom squeezed between them. Her cell phone did not work well here. This had been part of the plan, but now Annie realized how much she clung to that glass encased brick for comfort: scrolling through posts, checking email, texting her kids. No phone. No contact. Let it go—all of it. What if a bear attacked her? Even worse, what if a man attacked her? She was severed from the outside world, for the first time in maybe her whole life. Maybe it was actually safer here. No one would know what she did all day. She could invent it. Reinvent herself. What would she do all day? The excitement kept her up until 3 a.m., when exhaustion finally took over.

Is this a dream? I mean, right now, pinch yourself, Annie. Is it real? Annie pinched herself, started. Okay, maybe she had been dreaming, but this new place, this was a new reality, a new way of being. And to think, it had been here all along, as she made her way through the crowded city, trying to make some kind of impression, the trees had grown a tiny bit every year, until they were too big for a woman to get her arms around. That was the way to take up space: layer by layer, minute by minute.

Annie had forgotten to close the blinds in the night. So now, in the early morning, sunlight splayed across the bed, across her eyes. The sun didn't care that she had been up all night. It had places to go, things to do, trees to grow. Annie pulled the blinds closed, put her pillow over her head, and bought a few more minutes of something like rest.

Finally, she got up to look for coffee, to see where she was. There was a coffee maker on the counter, thank God. Annie was sure God was a caffeine addict too. I mean, look what she had done with the world, and on deadline! Definitely due to double espresso. Annie found the filters and the bag of decent coffee, and started her first task. The coffee was perfect, since there was nobody to tell her it was too strong. The view out the big window in the living room was strange and spectacular. There was a mist low under the pines, but up above, the sky was the bright blue that children color it with crayons. Annie wondered if she had been whisked to another dimension. She wondered if she had colored the sky a piercing light blue in elementary school. She wondered when she had stopped looking.

There was a knock on the door. Annie ran to grab her jeans from the bedroom floor and zipped up her gray hoody because she wasn't wearing a bra. The brochure had said nothing about visitors. She opened the door. The man was backlit by the sun that had nudged Annie awake just a few minutes before. He was a vision of something, but Annie wasn't sure what.

"Mornin'. You must be Ann? I'm Ranger Ben. I hear you'll be with us the whole month?" She confirmed his nametag, the green uniform, the clipboard he held with her name on the top of the calendar, a line drawn through the days of each week until the thirty-first.

"Um, yes, Ranger Ben, and it's Annie," she said, extending her hand. Ranger Ben shook it and nodded.

"Okay, Miss Annie, you call this number if you need anything. Otherwise, I'll leave you alone." He handed her his card.

"Thanks," Annie said. She hurried him out the door and locked it behind him. Would he leave her alone? Even here, she'd have to protect her space.

On the road, Annie had thought about her schedule, how she'd manage her time, but now, after her second cup of coffee and one of the bananas she had brought, she couldn't seem to get up from the kitchen chair. Was gravity stronger here? Maybe there was glue in the chair? Maybe she was just tired. Could a person be that tired? All the years she'd had, all the years she had left (who knows how many that might be), this very moment, they all fought each other, as if she had to choose only one to remember and hold on to before they all slipped away.

What did she expect from this place? Who knows? What do any of us expect when we get past what we have previously determined will be the "hard part" in life, and then find out that it's only the beginning? The beginning of what? Well, isn't that a good question? Isn't that what we're all wondering? What Annie expected that morning was a veil of peace to fall upon her, but of course that didn't happen.

Once the fog cleared, Annie pulled herself from the chair and lit out for the first trail she could find. The damp air enveloped her in a protective gauze. If she fell, it wouldn't hurt. Annie's feet created a rhythm as she walked, and she warmed up enough to take her fleece off and tie it around her waist. Her brain filled with all she hadn't done, things she should have reminded Oscar and Kate to keep track of while she was gone. The ticker tape of stress was picking up speed. She was a quarter mile down the path from the cabin when she finally remembered to look up. Oh, right—she was here. In a fucking forest. Let. it. go. But then she started singing the song. Sure, fine, I can sing "Let It Go," she thought. She took two deep breaths in without exhaling, then let all she held out in a whoosh. Oscar had taught her that trick the year he found meditation and yoga. He was always finding something. He was always looking up.

Annie looked around. She thought she saw a snake slither off the trail ahead, thought she heard its rustle. But there was no proof of the danger that might have been. No one praises you for saving them from invisible danger, but Annie had been doing that for people around her her whole life. Ingrates. They only said she was too anxious. Or worse, that she needed to relax. Didn't they know that her worrying had kept them alive, surrounded them in white light, kept them from so many certain calamities?

Forward. That's where she was going now. They would have to protect themselves from snakes on the path. Annie tried harder to be here now, as they say. But which moment was the real "now"? Where was "here"? She looked again. A worn to dirt and rocks path drew a light line through the greens and browns of the woods—tall pines, an oak here and there, some kind of maple, but Annie couldn't remember which. She used to know all the trees, whether they were full of leaves or bare. This was the biome of her childhood. She had grown up sixty or so miles from where she was stepping now, but she had taken a long and circuitous route back, through cities and suburbs, through labor and delivery, to plenty of soccer games and dance recitals, through a string of dead-end jobs that helped them get by, and finally, to the night Marco told the truth.

The truth was, he said, that he had never loved her. He had thought he had, you know, had wanted to, tried and tried—it had definitely been a burden to him—but now, he was fifty, goddamn it, and he meant to live his life, to love! Are you gonna laugh? Annie asked. See, damn it, you don't care about my feelings, my fulfillment, Marco said. Annie sat stunned at the dinner table, dirty plates filled with remnants of another meal she had cooked; he had eaten. She sat with the memory of who she had been when they had met thirty years before, compared herself to that free girl she had once known herself to be. The one who had let Marco move in after their second date and never leave. Until now. Oh. It suddenly occurred to Annie: this was him leaving. This was it. "No," Annie said, finally speaking out loud. "I don't care about your fulfillment. That's your job."

Marco had already booked a room at a hotel in town that night. He left dramatically, filling a couple of plastic grocery bags with some clothes, his razor, his toothbrush. You mind if I take one of these apples? He asked. Take it all, Annie said. I don't want any of it. This was another truth. She had never wanted all the things Marco had wanted. He had wanted to be an actor when they met, and look at that, Annie thought, he had been acting all along. He ought to get a fucking Academy Award for all the times he had told her he loved her, kissed her goodbye at the door. Goodbye, Marco, she said. Goodbye, he said, closing the door behind him. Closing all the doors.

She had to be a mile in on the trail now, right? A mile up the big hill that led to the top of the mountain. At least she felt like it had been a mile. She checked her fitness watch. Damn. That couldn't be just a half a mile. Could it? Time, space, distance, all the laws of physics, the idea that nothing is ever lost or gained, the speculation that it might all be an illusion, that the universe is full of black holes and tiny exoplanets, that our solar system wasn't the only one in the universe, those were the things that mattered now. That, and the fact that Annie was already feeling this in her quads. Her poor quads, neglected for so long. No wonder they were fighting back. We'll show you! her whole body seemed to be saying. That's what you get for letting that gym membership go, for sitting at a desk for so long, for keeping still and swallowing your words. Shut up, Annie said, to no one and everyone. I'm doing it now. I'm speaking now. And her muscles quieted and sort of obeyed in that mythical direction, the holy grail, forward.

The second morning, Annie woke a little earlier and started down a different trail. This one went downhill. She needed downhill today. Hopefully it was the "easy loop" the map said it was. She wanted to shake things up, to follow her whims every new day, but if you have spent most of your life creating routines, it's hard not to make one. Annie was determined that she would go with the fucking flow. Didn't she used to do that? It was really hard to remember what her days were actually like, thirty years before, in the time before Marco first ordered an espresso at the Empty Cup, the coffee shop she was working at, and she decided he was sophisticated. Voilà! was the first word she had said to him, and he had smiled. She kept saying voilà for the next thirty years because it reminded her of that very first connection, but he stopped seeing what it was she was presenting to him. He stopped lifting his head away from his work long enough to take a good look.

A group of hikers, in their twenties maybe, passed Annie on the trail and nodded. They carried packs for camping, they wore faded bandanas tied like headbands around their foreheads, they smelled a little like sweat and patchouli. Annie wanted to follow the scent of their youth, to eventually catch up, to join their conversation about weed dispensaries in New Jersey. She had been to one, she wanted to tell them! But they moved quickly down the trail toward the river, until their voices and laughter might have been birdsong, they were so closely linked.

The lactic acid in Annie's quads had dissipated once she started walking, but now, after two days in hiking boots, her feet were hurting. It was always something with this body. She got to the river, sat down on the bank, took off her boots and socks, and soaked her feet in the cool rushing water. A few light blue veins mapped her calves. She first thought of how they looked old, but then decided to think about the way the river of life was still flowing through her, like they said in yoga class. She closed her eyes. It had been a long time since she had felt this much physical pleasure, this much relief. She undressed and slid her whole body into the green of the river. She was floating on her back above the river rocks with her eyes closed when the hippie kids came to the bank. "Hey!" one of them said. "Look! It's Trail Mama!" Annie quickly crouched under the water. She didn't see Trail Mama, but she hoped they hadn't seen her. Then it dawned on her: They had named her. They had thought about who she might be. They had added her to their group as an imaginary matriarch. "Hey, Trail Mama!" One was waving at her. Couldn't they see she was naked? They didn't seem to mind, and maybe she didn't look so bad, maybe there was a way she could be beautiful. The hippie kids threw off their clothes, letting them land anywhere, as if they didn't care whether they found them again. Annie fought the urge to get out of the water and gather them for them. She was mesmerized by their perfect skin, their perfect abandon. She covered her breasts with one arm and waved to the kids with the other. Then she changed her mind and waved with both arms. Who cares if they saw her naked? Annie had noticed her body was almost invisible. Plus, she wasn't even herself anymore. She was Trail Mama, and Trail Mama was definitely a skinny dipper.

The kids, Cackle, Tom-tom, and Wispy, wanted to know all about her, but not the way most people did. They didn't care who she was related to. To them, she was clearly traveling alone. They wanted to know how long she had been on the trail, where she had slept last night, if she had any weed to share, why she was here. They wanted to know if she had had awesome dreams. "I just got here," she said. "But yeah, I think I had some awesome dreams. I don't remember them, but I woke up feeling good."

"You see, Cackle, that's what I was talking about!" Wispy said, slapping the water with her hands. "It's the feeling it leaves you with that matters, not what you remember."

"Okay. I feel that," Cackle said, then he laughed and, well, Annie realized how he got his trail name.

They waded in the water, talking and splashing in the sunlight until their fingers pruned. Finally, Annie pulled herself up onto the bank and let the sun dry her. She was, for once, not ashamed of her body. What a strange sensation, to just let yourself be human and nothing else. She stayed there a while before she re-dressed. The kids scampered up the bank and found their clothes too. They put their packs back on and gave her peace signs.

"All the love!" Wispy said. "Take it easy, Trail Mama," Tom-tom said.

"You too," Annie said. "Happy trails." That made Cackle laugh, and they chattered together as they headed back down the trail.

The shadows were getting longer. It was getting deep into the afternoon. Annie would have to start back now if she was going to get back before dark. She climbed up the bank to the trail and picked up the first long thin branch she could find to use as a walking stick. It made her feel regal—a staff for Queen Annie. She hummed to herself. That damn song would not get out of her head. A deer suddenly ran straight across the trail ahead of her, so close it almost brushed against her. Her heart raced, and she couldn't catch her breath. She didn't want to be startled anymore, not after the way Marco had stunned her. Double breath, then big exhale she thought, grateful for Oscar's penchant for optimizing himself. Grateful that her children still spoke to her, unlike her friend Marlene, whose children judged every word that came out of their mother's mouth until she had stopped talking to them as a defense. Grateful for the hippie kids and their unhurried joy.

As she walked, Annie found small sticks on the trail and put them in her pockets. She liked to keep things neat, and they littered the trail. A storm must have come through a few days before. Funny how the trees kept a record of the weather. The sticks she picked weren't special. They could have come from any tree—didn't matter. When her pockets were full, Annie pulled up the hem of her T-shirt to make a pouch and gathered more sticks. Back in the cabin, she dumped them all on the coffee table. They covered the tabletop. She should make something with them. She couldn't throw them away after all the time it had taken the trees to make them. She couldn't do what the song said. Release was harder than grasping. Annie knew what she had to do. She went to bed and tried to dream the awesome dreams Wispy had talked about. She wanted to wake up feeling great. She wanted to have visions. A text woke her after midnight. Annie had almost forgotten about her phone; she had also forgotten to silence it. She was losing track of time, days. A stray signal must have gotten through.

Do you know where my winter coat is? Marco asked. The gall, Annie thought. First, why was he up at midnight, second, why was he asking her? Oh, right. He had always asked her, at least for the last thirty years. She was supposed to be the keeper of all things. The alpha and the omega of the home. His coat-check girl too.

No idea, she wrote back, even though she knew it was in the back of the big closet in Kate's room, where she always stored their winter coats. Was it cold enough for a winter coat? Annie silenced her phone and tried to go back to sleep, but anger had surged through her and now she was wide awake, rehashing everything: all he had said, all the times he had lied, all the times she should have seen where this would all eventually go. She got up and sat for a while on the couch next to the pile of sticks on the table, then she brushed the pile to the floor with a sweep of her arm. Was she crazy? She felt crazy. But at least, she thought, she felt something.

 It was around 4 a.m. when Annie finally went to bed again. This time she slept without worrying whether or not she would dream. She had moved the coffee table and stacked the sticks in a circle on the floor, wedging couch pillows around them. You could call it a nest, sure, but for now, Annie was calling it a project. She hadn't made anything in years, since she had contemplated declaring an art major in the second semester of her sophomore year of college.

"You could be an art major," Marco had said. "Or you could get a business degree and still be an artist in your spare time. Then you don't have to starve."

This had sounded so smart, so right, so protective. But there would never be anything called spare time. Not once they were married, not once the kids came, not once she had given her life to managing other people's spreadsheets. Annie's friend Sarah Chandler, who now went by one name: Sahara, who had never once considered being a business major; she was making art for a living, showing her paintings all over the state.

In the morning, Annie took her coffee mug and carefully climbed over the edge of the sticks to sit in the middle. A few sticks fell away and she restacked them. Inside the nest, Annie felt better somehow. Free? Safe? Maybe yes, but maybe just more like the Annie she had once been. The one who made art.

She needed more sticks, so she dressed and hit the trail. This time there was a family on the trail. Annie lagged behind, trying to lose them, but their small daughter was interested in her stick collecting and started collecting her own. Annie had a bag this time, and it was filling quickly. She wished the little girl would leave. Her parents kept looking at Annie, and calling the girl, Jamaica, back. It was clear that they were a little worried about her proximity to Annie, the stick collector, the wild woman, the strange bird.

"Jamaica!" they called. This time, they meant it. The little girl finally ran to them, dropping her sticks along the way. Annie picked them up once Jamaica and her family were out of view.

Was she someone to be feared? Annie didn't think so. Maybe she should have showered, brushed her hair? No. Maybe she wanted to scare them off. This is who she was, a collector, a tidier of the forest, a creator. She moved down the trail. Trail Mama, yes. That is who she was now. She had the urge to post that on Instagram, maybe with a photo of her hiking boots, but she had forgotten her phone. For a moment she was panicked. She never forgot her phone—what if something happened? What if her children needed her? What if Marco—okay, it was a good thing she had forgotten her phone. She could find her way without it. Annie kept hiking for another mile or so. It felt like a mile, so this time, with nothing to prove her wrong, she called it a mile. She had a sandwich in her day pack, some chips, an apple. She found a boulder in the woods to sit on and ate.

Annie saw something through the trees—another cabin? She thought she had gotten beyond civilization out here, only a mile in, but obviously not. She would have to go farther. Let it—no. Annie wouldn't sing it again. Instead, she started humming a Grateful Dead song. She had liked them a lot before she met Marco. He had told her they were uncool, had introduced her to Indie bands, but a person could get tired of Radiohead. A person could learn to dread the Smiths. *Walking through the tall trees. Going where the wind blows*, she hummed.

Without her phone, Annie didn't know what time it was. She wanted to finish the loop, so she kept hiking. Who could get lost in a loop? She saw that the sky was darkening, but she didn't know how quickly the storm would come. Suddenly, it was pouring rain, as if she had willed it to start. Had she? Could her thoughts control the weather? Who knew what she was capable of? She closed her eyes and tried to think of sunshine, but the rain came harder. Maybe the universe wasn't always listening to her thoughts like some Google algorithm. Maybe she was not in charge of anything, least of all the weather.

Annie held the plastic bag full of sticks over her head in an attempt at shelter. It didn't work. Maybe she should empty the bag into her pack and put the plastic bag over her hair? But the pack was full of sticks too, and Annie didn't want to—you know. She clutched the bag to her chest and ran down the trail, back to her cabin, to her project.

She was soaked but safe. Her wet boots left puddles everywhere she stepped. It made her laugh.

Annie peeled her clothes off and got into bed naked. She would stack the sticks in the morning. She would have awesome dreams. She would know exactly what this felt like, to be free for rings and rings of time.

The next day, when Annie set out, she had a plan. She brought two empty bags, a sandwich, and some water. She had brushed her hair in case she saw other people. She hiked for a while. Gathered sticks. Ate. No one passed. She guessed it was a Monday or maybe a Tuesday. No one hiked early in the week. Annie's feet propelled her forward. She thought she heard a deer, so she stood still for one breath, two breaths, three. No deer. She yelled her own name into the air. No answer. Her pockets filled with sticks and she imagined the structure she could build, how it might sit one day in the middle of a white room, so other people could look at it and wonder what it meant. Was that what she wanted? Annie moved forward and deeper into herself, and it surprised her when the sun got low so fast. She thought she had only gone a few miles. Maybe four? How could you tell how far you had gone without the world to tell you? How could you tell when night would fall? Maybe this was a loop. Maybe not. Annie kept going anyway. She could sleep protected by trees, like the kids on the trail. She could bathe in the river. She could keep moving and let the trail take her where it wanted. She could find her way back to the beginning.

Say Goodbye to the Boob

Susan Jensen

I was chastised the other day for making people uncomfortable when I said I couldn't wait to get my boob off at the end of the day.

I didn't say it to make people uncomfortable. It's just been a fact of my life for so long. And a fact of life for millions of other women who are breast cancer survivors who wear a prosthesis, a fake breast made of silicone.

But I've been thinking about why that comment made me so angry. And why it makes people uncomfortable.

It's because we don't talk about it.

So many survivors feel like less of a woman because we're missing a breast. Somehow it's almost worse than losing another body part, like an arm or a leg. Breasts are so venerated in our culture and so tied in with our sexual identity, that it's difficult for anyone to imagine a woman losing that part of herself.

So we don't talk about it. We have horrific surgeries to cover it up or wear an uncomfortable prosthesis to make it look like it never happened.

But it's time to start talking about it. So here goes.

I was diagnosed with breast cancer while I was still nursing my second child. It was a 6 cm tumor. I had a modified radical mastectomy and follow-up chemotherapy. I later learned I should not have lived past six months. So the surgery saved my life.

I have worn a 2-pound rubber prosthesis in public ever since in order to make other people comfortable with my appearance. I have made other people feel comfortable while being uncomfortable myself with that sweaty thing strapped to my chest. And there was also a certain amount of shame attached to not having a breast and feeling the need to wear that thing.

Some men couldn't get past it, but real men could. And did.

As of today, I am done feeling any type of shame. I am proud of the surgery that saved my life and kept me alive so I could work 24/7 and raise my children as a single mother with no child support. I am proud of that scar that goes from the middle of my chest all the way around to my side under my arm. It is beautiful. It is my battle scar.

People have asked why I haven't had reconstructive surgery. At first, I was so busy raising my children that it didn't matter. After that, it just seemed stupid. And dangerous.

There are two types of reconstructive surgery: implants and flap.

An implant is a rubber breast–shaped balloon filled with either a saline solution or a gel. It is inserted under the skin of the mastectomy scar after a skin expander has expanded the skin over a period of time. The Mayo Clinic explains the risks:

"Breast reconstruction with a breast implant carries the possibility of complications, including

Breasts that don't match each other in size or appearance (asymmetry)
Breast pain
Implant rupture or deflation
Poor healing of incisions
Increased risk of future breast surgery to replace or remove the breast implant
Changes in breast sensation
Infection
Bleeding
Scar tissue that forms and compresses the implant and breast tissue into a hard, unnatural shape (capsular contracture)
Risks associated with anesthesia
Increased risk of a rare immune system cancer called anaplastic large cell lymphoma (ALCL) that's associated with textured breast implants

Correcting any of these complications may require additional surgery."

Flap surgery opens up the scar, takes a chunk of tissue off the stomach or buttocks and places it inside the scar, creating two scars on the breast instead of one, and a sizable scar on the stomach or buttocks. The aureole of the nipple is taken from vaginal tissue and sewn on the mound. Or it can be tattooed on and a chunk of the stomach or buttocks that was used to create the mound can be pulled out to create a nipple. A nipple can also be created by taking a piece of the cartilage at the back of the ear and sewing it on top of the aureole. The Mayo Clinic explains those risks also:

"Breast reconstruction with flap surgery is a major procedure and carries with it the possibility of significant complications, including

Changes in breast sensation
Prolonged time in surgery and under anesthesia
Extended recovery and healing time

Poor wound healing

Fluid collection (seroma)

Infection

Bleeding

Tissue death (necrosis) due to insufficient blood supply

Loss of sensation at the tissue donor site

Abdominal wall hernia or weakness"

Frankenstein-ian. And for what? Just to make others comfortable?

I applaud women if they choose reconstructive surgery. It's an individual choice. I don't condemn them for choosing it any more than anyone should condemn me for not wearing a prosthesis to make you comfortable.

Or for daring to even mention it.

We are a breast obsessed culture. If you would like a breast to play with, I have a rubber boob you can have. You can have it, but you cannot have me.

As of today, you will just have to be uncomfortable with my appearance, because I am never wearing that ridiculous prosthesis again to make you comfortable. My comfort comes first. Finally. Sorry. Not sorry. But you will just have to live with it. I have. I've had some wonderful relationships and a full and rich life. But I'm tired of making you comfortable at my expense.

I am so much more than a blob of fat on my chest.

Because I am fabulous without it.

Not expecting to fly. Flying anyway.

Erin Robertson

in response to Expecting to Fly *by Susan Goldstein*

he hasn't yet noticed
her tattooed wings
or how her feet
have stopped touching
the kitchen floor

his nose is in a book
not the crook of her neck

she's pupating
unstoppable
everything in her's dissolving
she's losing legs and growing
luminous iridescent scales

he hadn't quite registered
how still she stood
for just how long
while her insides melted

there's nothing to be done now
she didn't ask to change
it was something outside her
the light the stars the calendar page
the lack of his hand in hers

she's not sure what she's in for
can't see how this lot will look
when she's airborne and weightless
hitting escape velocity
launched on her own.

Feral

Suzanne Chick

I'm noticing the older I get, the more feral I'm becoming.

Sometimes, days will go by before I remember to brush my hair.

Makeup is not an option unless I work or I have to be out in

civilization,

which I avoid if at all possible.

I don't know if my clothes match

my socks are ragged and should all be thrown out.

They're looking rough.

I eat and drink too fast.

And I'm always in a hurry to go here or there

I'm constantly indulging in things.

Books, ice cream, hiking, floating on the lake, daydreaming.

I rarely plan my day and if I do, I don't stick to it anyway

I think I've done my time as a tame woman

So off to the forest I go.

The Cambium Layer

Elinor Davis

"There are two ways to get to Stewart Island," the waiter says in response to a question he must get often. "By air or sea—twenty minutes of terror or an hour of hell." He plunks a steaming plate of mussels and Bluff oysters on the table and elaborates on the options: a six-passenger airplane from Invercargill, a helicopter from Bluff, or a catamaran ferry that departs twice a day from a dock two minutes up the road from the Shearwater Hotel, where Helen has booked a room.

Remembering her mother's admonition—*If you want to live a long life, eat your vegetables and stay out of small planes*—Helen decides to take the boat. She has upped her veggie intake in recent years (though her mother Flora, the most prodigious baker in Gompers, Kansas, counted her famous rhubarb pie in the vegetable category). But she's never before now had the opportunity to eschew a ride in a small plane, like the one that plunged into an Iowa cornfield killing Buddy Holly, Ritchie Valens, and the Big Bopper when she was a child. The boat feels like a proactive choice for her health.

The desk clerk at the Shearwater (who along with his wife turns out to also be the owner, manager, bellhop, and breakfast cook) affirms her choice. "That ferry is a marvel, all the latest safety equipment and sturdy as a battleship. The last one broke to bits after a few months, so they had this one specially designed and built to survive the Foveaux Strait. Only boat like it in the world," he claims. While signing the register, Helen hears him tell another guest that the plane ride is "quite the thrill." Just humoring his customer, she thinks, confident she chose the safer conveyance.

Glancing at the wall behind the counter, she is startled to see a clock with the numbers marching backwards (proceeding left from the 12 instead of right) and the second hand running counterclockwise. *Ah, a "down-under" joke.* The proprietors and their three small children live in a few cramped rooms behind the desk area, visible through a half-open door. The spacious lobby, with its TV and overstuffed sofas, apparently doubles as their living room. Several fortyish women with local accents are sipping coffee and gossiping about someone on the TV while kids chase each other around the furniture in some make-believe game. The women seem to know each other, and Helen can't tell if they are hotel guests or the owners' friends on a social visit. She feels as if she has inadvertently walked into a stranger's home, a domestic vignette in which she, the road-weary traveler, has no place.

This trip to New Zealand was an impulse purchase, a birthday present to herself at her children's urging. "Mom, you should get away and relax, do something nice for yourself," they insisted in calls and emails from their distant homes, concerned for her state of mind. *Although not concerned enough to come visit or invite me to vacation with them,* Helen couldn't help thinking. She had spent six exhausting years as a caregiver through her own mother's decline into dementia and heart failure. When her mother's body finally gave out three months ago, Helen experienced grief and relief in almost equal measure, and guilt about the relief. Her already shaky marriage to a self-absorbed man with an over-fondness for Irish whiskey had also fallen victim to the strain of those years, and once she'd settled her mother's affairs, she felt empty, drained, and devoid of purpose. No one needed her anymore. She wanted only to sleep and dream of happier times, when she was young, bubbling with energy and hope. *What kind of example is that to set—life must go on!* she imagined her mother scolding. After all, she would not want her children to collapse into despair or ennui when she dies. She must rally, be a role model of resilience. For their sake, she will attempt to enjoy herself. Her mother would be proud.

So, she has taken a leave of absence from her bank teller job to go somewhere lovely, somewhere utterly different from the featureless plains of home. A place where she doesn't know a soul and can spend her days exactly as she pleases without having to accommodate anyone else's needs or wishes. She wants wild beauty and exotic animals, but in a setting where she feels safe traveling alone on her first solo vacation. New Zealand meets all criteria and does not disappoint. The people here even speak mostly understandable English. If they didn't drive on the wrong side of the road, she would have rented a car. But trains, buses, and boats have efficiently taken her all over the South Island, from alpine mountains to rain forests to pristine beaches and turquoise lakes, to deep fjords lined with waterfalls, and caves lit by glow-worms. She has seen penguins and parrots, sea elephants and sea lions, mentholated trees, odd knobby fruits, and crimson flowers unknown on the Kansas prairie. Being a passenger frees her to drink in the passing scenery and everywhere she looks could be a postcard.

Helen settles into her modest quarters on the second floor of the Shearwater. In contrast to the Art Deco architecture of the hotel building itself, the room reminds her of a 1950s American tract home—chintz curtains, twin beds with blue chenille bedspreads, a tall dresser, matching two-tier nightstands with elevated shelves for glasses, alarm clock, a magazine. Large pink flowers repeat themselves across the green-bordered carpet, which gives way to white tile at the bathroom door. She takes a scalding shower to banish the chill of the walk from the restaurant through a drizzle and wind barreling in off the Foveaux Strait.

Her Midwestern Protestant upbringing does not allow her to indulge in hedonistic pleasures without some redeeming purpose. Hence, to derive maximum educational value from this vacation, she had studied the history, flora, and fauna of New Zealand, first on the internet, then in mail-ordered books now taking up precious space and weight in her luggage. She wraps the extra blanket over her nightgown like a shawl and climbs into the bed nearest the radiator to read up on Stewart Island, a "bird-watcher's paradise," an "unspoiled gem off the beaten tourist path." Called Rakiura, "land of glowing skies" in the Maori language, it lies in the Tasman Sea, 30 kilometers beyond the southern tip of the South Island. Next stop, Antarctica. She drifts off to the sound of wind rattling the windows and whooshing up the alley behind the hotel.

After a breakfast of muffins, poached egg, stewed feijoas, and strong coffee, Helen tows her suitcase up the road to the ferry dock and buys a one-way ticket. Not sure how long I'll stay, she tells the clerk. Usually a meticulous planner, she surprises herself with this spark of spontaneity.

The ferry interior resembles an airliner cabin, but much wider, with a higher ceiling, more comfortable seats, and a lot more legroom. No need for overhead bins because the luggage has been stowed in the hold below. Like a plane, each seatback pouch contains emergency instructions and a wax-lined paper bag. Smiling young attendants in navy blue uniforms greet passengers, and when all are seated, they demonstrate the safety features and point out lifejackets and lifeboats.

The reason for the motion sickness bags soon becomes apparent. Minutes after gliding away from the dock, the ferry is lurching side to side while slamming into endless oncoming waves that rock the cabin back and forth and sideways simultaneously without pause. Passengers groan and grab for the bags, including an elderly man next to Helen who moans, "I'm an old Navy man—I never got seasick on the ocean, but here I am tossing my breakfast on a ferry boat." Attendants appear with wet cloths, which they apply to foreheads and napes of necks. They murmur soothing phrases, trade used bags for fresh ones, encourage the queasy to close their eyes rather than watch the churning water and bouncing horizon through the huge windows.

Helen feels oddly exhilarated. Better than a carnival ride, it's the most intensely physical experience she's had in years, driving out all concerns beyond the desire to avoid vomiting in public. She recalls reading that the 16-mile-wide Foveaux Strait is one of the roughest stretches of water in the world. Its flat, shallow bottom exaggerates the tidal action from the seas beyond, making navigation especially treacherous, and it is frequently assaulted by howling storms. She goes outside to stand at the railing and feel the wind and mist on her face, smell the salt air, and watch the petrels, cormorants, and albatross wheel and soar behind the boat.

After the invigorating "hour of hell," the ferry slides to rest at Halfmoon Bay in Oban, the only settlement on the island, and Helen debarks to call the B&B she reserved. "Just call when you arrive and I'll pop down to pick you up," the owner Marjorie had written. "It's walkable, but we're up a hill and you'll have luggage." The old Navy man totters down the ramp behind her, still looking green and embarrassed. "Guess I've lost my sea legs," he says with a wan smile. He also makes a phone call, and when the B&B owner arrives ten minutes later, they realize they are staying at the same place.

"Are you together, then?" asks Marjorie. "I have you booked in separate rooms."

"Oh, no, we just met on the ferry," Helen quickly answers.

"I'm Jerry, by the way," the Navy man says.

The old station wagon chugs up a winding gravel road past lush shrubs and trees that mostly obscure the occasional house. Up a driveway, the Cairn Craig Bed & Breakfast sprawls across a level clearing on the hill, surrounded by jungle still glistening from the latest rain shower. It appears to be a bungalow onto which additions have been grafted in every direction to enlarge its capacity for tourists. Three levels, with small balconies on stilts jutting from each guest room.

A broad tree stump squats in the yard surrounded by sections of its trunk, waiting to be split for firewood. Helen sees the clearly defined rings indicating the tree's growth over many years and remembers an illustration from her college botany textbook, labeled with the five parts of a tree. *Bark > phloem > cambium > xylem > wood. Under the protective outer bark, the cambium is a very thin layer of tissue, sometimes only one cell thick. It produces new growth and is the only part of a tree that is alive.* Before reading this, she had thought of the leaves and blossoms as being "alive." But no. Only the cambium layer. If the cambium is breached and exposed all the way around the circumference ("girdled," as the book quaintly put it), it dries out and the whole tree dies because it can no longer transport nutrients from the leaves down to the roots. She wonders if the tree was cut down because some pest or disease had girdled and killed it. She wonders if she has a cambium layer herself and what kind of shape it's in.

"Let me make you some tea," Marjorie says after they wrestle their bags up the stairs to their rooms. She shows them to a small table by sliding glass doors leading to a terrace. Along with the tray of tea and muffins, she brings a bowl of peanuts. Within seconds after they sit down, three green kaka parrots light on the wooden deck and stare pointedly at Helen as if to say, *Where is our lunch?* Marjorie slides open the door and tosses a nut that is quickly snatched by the nearest kaka. "They have you well-trained," Jerry says, throwing out more peanuts. "The birds outnumber us here, so we just give them whatever they want," Marjorie admits.

The trees beyond ring with the calls of tui, kereru pigeons, bell birds, magpies, and parakeets that dart and swoop across the hillside. *I must get out my bird book,* Helen thinks. That evening, Marjorie sees her in the guest lounge studying her *Field Guide to the Birds of New Zealand* and asks, "Are you a birder?"

"No, but there are so many different birds here, I want to identify all the ones I see and write them down." This idea cheers her somehow, an assignment, a purpose.

Jerry wanders in and peeks over her shoulder. "You'll see hundreds of those sooty shearwaters, mutton birds they call them. And the albatross are huge."

"You'll want to take the trip to Ulva Island," Marjorie says. "It's one of the uninhabited islands where the introduced predators have been eradicated, like rats and weasels brought by settlers. You can see kiwi and other birds found nowhere else in the world."

De facto traveling companions again, the next day Helen and Jerry take the boat to Ulva Island. At the small visitor center, a sign invites them to "Meet Sirocco, the Kakapo Ambassador and Official Spokesbird for Conservation!" They have stumbled upon a temporary exhibit of a very rare bird, a kakapo or "night parrot." A ranger explains that kakapos once lived all over New Zealand but had long been thought to be extinct. Then a few were found in the 1970s on Stewart Island and brought to several of the small islands nearby where the Department of Conservation conducts a breeding program that aims to bring them back to sustainable numbers. Currently, only 150 individuals are known to exist, and they only breed every two to five years, depending on environmental conditions.

Flightless and nocturnal with no natural enemies until humans and rats arrived, the kakapo nests on the ground and forages for food at night, favoring the red berries of the rimu tree when available, the ranger tells them. "It's the largest, heaviest, and probably the longest-lived parrot on earth. If you want to see Sirocco, stay until dark when he's awake. You can take the last boat back."

Helen wants to see the kakapo and Jerry seems inclined to stick with Helen, so they spend the afternoon meandering along the track through thick woods, catching glimpses of birds with their binoculars and looking them up in Helen's book. She warms to the self-assigned task of recording all the birds, animals, and plants she sees in New Zealand and regrets not starting sooner. She imagines preparing a slide show for family and friends back home, perhaps a presentation at church or the library, something to justify this extravagant trip. Thanks to the digital camera and extra memory cards she bought, she's already taken more than 2,000 photos, not to mention the postcards and pamphlets from everywhere she stops.

As the sun sinks into the sea, they sit on a bench near the dock and make a picnic supper of the sandwiches and oranges Marjorie had kindly provided, since there are no vendors on Ulva. They drink from water bottles, careful not to leave any litter on this island that must be kept as free of human contamination as possible so the wildlife may flourish. "This is when the fireflies would be coming out back home," Helen says.

"Where's home?"

"Kansas, a little podunk town, nothing to compare with the wonders of New Zealand. What about you?" She has wondered about Jerry's accent, which sounds too Kiwi to be American and too American to be Kiwi.

"Virginia, originally, but the US Navy sent me here forty years ago and I never left. Married a local girl . . . I lost her last year, been sort of at loose ends . . . Never been down to these islands before, just thought I'd see if I was missing anything."

"And what's the verdict?"

"Great scenery, but I'm not looking forward to the ferry back to Bluff. I've had enough of the Foveaux Strait."

Helen refrains from mentioning that she found the ferry ride exciting. "I hope the Strait is calmer on your way back. It's pretty dark now. Shall we see if the kakapo is awake?"

They stow the water bottles and bag of orange rinds in Helen's tote bag and make their way back to the visitor center. Though they'd read the pamphlet about the Critically Endangered Giant Parrot, it did not quite prepare them for the sight of Sirocco in the flesh. Entering a dimly lit enclosure, they first see a tan owl-like face with bright black eyes and a large, thick, ivory-colored beak curving down against a receding chin and tan breast. His crown and the rest of his stout body are covered in short, soft, mossy green feathers mottled with brown and yellow, creating a perfect camouflage against the leafy forest floor where the kakapo evolved. His thick thighs sprout long powerful claws that cling to a low branch where he roosted during the day. Though he cannot fly, he's a good runner and tree-climber. Two feet long and nearly as tall, it is his size that stuns them most at close quarters—he would dwarf the perky kakas that frequent Marjorie's terrace. Sirocco gazes at the humans with what seems a shy curiosity, cocking his head from side to side. He jumps off the branch and spreads his wings to break the fall, then waddles along the ground casting occasional sidelong glances at the enrapt visitors.

Helen feels light-headed and realizes she has been holding her breath, not wanting to move lest she alarm this creature from another time. *I wonder if he knows he's one of the last of his kind.* The ranger explains that Sirocco got a respiratory infection when he was only a few weeks old and was taken from his mother's nest for treatment to save his life. "He had to be hand-raised and therefore he imprinted on his human caregivers instead of learning how to relate to other kakapos, including proper mating behavior." Thus rendered unlikely to ever breed, and being comfortable around humans, he now travels around New Zealand to raise awareness about conservation and the project to save his species from extinction. Sirocco lets out a loud shrieking *skraak* as if to affirm the ranger's account.

Helen can't decide if the huge bird is exotic or homely, or both; magnificent or poignant, or both. But watching him putter and scratch about his pen looking for seeds, bark, berries, and roots, she is stricken and moved in a way she can only compare to what she felt when she first saw her firstborn child. A stirring, like sap rising in a long dormant tree, tingles beneath her skin.

"I read in your pamphlet that the recovery program uses volunteers," Helen says to the ranger. "Do you need anyone right now?"

"Actually, a new crew starts next week on Codfish Island. All the slots were filled, but I heard that the volunteer cook just cancelled."

"I can cook," Helen hears herself say. The ranger hands her a card with a phone number and website.

"You better call them. The online volunteer application form may not be posted right now."

Jerry eyes her curiously as she watches Sirocco, a plucky creature unaware of the existential threat to the future of his tribe. She lingers until the ranger closes the exhibit for the night.

As they board the boat, the sky begins to shimmer and glow, bright green at the horizon blending into magenta and violet higher up. Helen gasps and gapes. "The southern lights," Jerry says. "Aren't they something?" She has read about the aurora, of course, but this vibrating light show is more spectacular than she could have imagined. They motor back to Oban in silent awe.

It is late when they reach the B&B, but Helen uses the guest computer in the lounge to read through the kakapo project website. Early the next morning, she calls the number the ranger gave her and someone emails her the application form.

Over the next three days, Helen and Jerry take a minibus tour of Stewart Island, visit the small museum, cruise the bay in a glass-bottom boat, dine in the few restaurants, hike the hills, stroll the waterfront, and explore several lovely deserted beaches. On day four, Jerry pays his bill and loads his suitcase in Marjorie's car for the drive to the ferry. "If you get tired of cooking for the parrot people, you're welcome to visit me in Christchurch," he tells Helen. "My house has a guest apartment," he adds, lest she think him too presumptuous. "I'll show you the sights of the city." She accepts the proffered slip of paper with his address and number but is noncommittal regarding a visit, feeling no need to see a city just now. She rides along to the dock and waves goodbye to Jerry as he stoically boards the boat under a steady drizzle.

From Cairn Craig, Helen launches a flotilla of emails. She informs her children she will be staying in New Zealand indefinitely; deputizes a realtor friend to put her possessions in storage and sublet her apartment; resigns her job and applies online for Social Security. She extends her B&B stay until the day she can join the kakapo project and buys some rubber rain boots and a sturdy lime-green slicker from the little general store in Oban. She can almost feel her cambium layer absorbing moisture from the air and reviving itself.

In her new raingear, she takes a long walk through the verdant hills and down to Ringaringa Beach, where hers are the only human footprints on this curve of white sand sprinkled with cockle shells and driftwood. Oystercatchers skitter along the surf while overhead, terns and mollymawks glide and squawk. Under the water, sea stars wriggle and fish weave through dancing forests of kelp. And somewhere beyond this shore is a little island of giant parrots perched on the brink of oblivion, and a handful of humans nudging them back from the edge.

Contributors

VICTORIA CASTAÑEDA was raised in rural Alabama by a family of undocumented migrant women from Ciudad Juarez, Mexico. After more than five years working with migrants and refugees in Mexico, Greece, Serbia, and the United States, she is now working on an intergenerational memoir, which centers oral history interviews with the women in her family. The interviews chronicle decades of family stories about their experiences with single motherhood, gender-based violence, criminal activity, and undocumented immigration. By allowing the women in her family to speak for themselves, Victoria immerses readers in their search for autonomy and dignity within and despite oppressive systems. Alongside these interviews, Victoria draws from her professional and academic background in migration to contextualize her family's stories while taking the reader on her personal journey in hearing them. Victoria holds a BA from Stanford University and an MSc from the University of Oxford. She currently lives in Mexico City, where she supports international humanitarian organizations in improving direct services to migrants.

LAUREN HAYES grew up in Huntsville, Alabama, where she studied psychology and gender studies. She and her wife share their home in the DC metro area with an extraordinarily spoiled dog. She began writing poetry as a teen and is in the process of editing her first novel. When she isn't writing, she spends entirely too much time watching horror films and buying books about witches. In addition to *TulipTree Review*, her poetry has appeared in *Bella Grace Magazine*. You can follow her on Instagram (@LHayesWrites).

ESTHER RA alternates between California and Seoul, South Korea. She is the author of *A Glossary of Light and Shadow* (Diode Editions, 2023, recipient of the Diode Full-Length Book Prize) and *book of untranslatable things* (Grayson Books, 2018). Her work has been published in *American Literary Review*, *Boulevard*, *Rattle*, *The Rumpus*, *Bellingham Review*, *PBQ*, and *Korea Times*, among others. She has been the recipient of numerous awards, including the Pushcart Prize, 49th Parallel Award for Poetry, Women Writing War Poetry Award, and Sweet Lit Poetry Award. Esther is currently a JD candidate at Stanford Law School. Learn more at estherra.com.

ROSIE COHAN is an award-winning travel writer. She has traveled in seventy countries, including seventeen trips to Turkey, her "home away from home." Her descriptions and photographs of the natural world, interesting characters, and different cultural traditions not only present the uniqueness of various countries but illustrate the universality of the human experience. She also writes about her experiences as a solo woman exploring the world. Her website is www.Rosiecohan.com. Her work has been published on GeoEx.com, Besttravelwriting.com, CheeseProfessor.com, BATW.org/magazine, and in anthologies including *Stories That Need to Be Told*, *AboutPlace.org*, and *Travel Stories of Wonder and Change*. Several of her stories have won the Solas Award from Traveler's Tales and have been featured on their website, Travelerstales.com. Rosie lives and writes in Berkeley, California—truly a world unto itself.

MARY PAULSON's writing has appeared in a host of journals, most recently in *Door Is a Jar*, *The Closed Eye Open*, the *Corvus Review*, *Spank the Carp*, *Unleash Lit*, *The Opiate*, *The Café Review*, and *The Rumen*. Her poems have been anthologized in multiple publications. She was recently awarded third prize for her poem "Pantoum at Sixteen" by the Kent and Sussex Poetry Society. She was also a joint winner in *The Letter Review*'s Poetry 2024 contest. In 2023, she won a place in the *Writer's Digest* annual awards for her free-verse poem "Go." Her chapbook, *Paint the Window Open*, was published in 2021 by Kelsay Press. She lives in Naples, Florida. You can follow her on Facebook (facebook.com /mary.paulson.35) and Instagram (instagram.com/my_tigerlily).

KAYLA HEINZ (she/her) currently lives along the Clark Fork River in Montana, with ties to the Great Lakes and the Pacific Coast. Like cupping ocean water in your hand, her writing grasps at the finite experiences that constitute the infinite and our connection with it. Cherishing these brief beauties and their equal griefs, her work returns again and again like the tide to themes of companionship. She is a recent college graduate working in wildlife conservation, and her poems have previously appeared in *Sixfold*. You can follow her writing at kaylaheinze.substack.com.

Creative nonfiction and place-based author MOLLY MURFEE pens her prose from the rural heart of the Southern Rocky Mountains. She writes the *Earth Muffin Memos* column and blog, fostering environmental and social change, and has over 500 published articles, from local venues to national magazines such as *Mountain Journal*, the *Mountain Gazette*, and *Powder Magazine*. Professionally Molly teaches field-based national and international courses in nature writing, environmental literature, mythology, and environmental philosophy at Western Colorado University through the Clark Family School of Environment and Sustainability, the Honors Program, and the Teacher Institute. As a creative activist, she codirects her local Autumn Equinox celebration, generating earth-honoring and community-building practices through storytelling, mythmaking, public art, and street theater. Molly has been honored as a 2024 Aldo and Estella Leopold Writing Resident; 2023 Mountain Words Local Writer-in-Residence; 2022 Annie Dillard Award for Creative Nonfiction finalist; 2022 Bread Loaf Environmental Writers' Conference contributor; and 2019 Colorado Creative Industries Career Advancement Award recipient, among other honors. "The Procedure" contains ideas for her first book, *The Adventure of Home*. This creative nonfiction work re-members our indigeneity to this Earth through braided lyrical narratives unraveling our destructive foundations of colonialism and reweaving mythologies of a sacred wild.

KINSALE DRAKE (Diné) is a winner of the 2023 National Poetry Series for her debut poetry collection *The Sky Was Once a Dark Blanket* (University of Georgia Press, 2024). Her work has appeared in *Poetry Magazine*, *Poets.org*, *Best New Poets*, *Black Warrior Review*, *Nylon*, *Teen Vogue*, and elsewhere. She is the founder of NDN Girls Book Club, a literary nonprofit for Indigenous youth.

EDDI SALADO is an award-winning California-based poet and retired educator. She has a degree in creative writing from College of Creative Studies, University of California Santa Barbara, and a master's degree in composition and literacy also from University of California. Her poems and articles have appeared in several publications. She currently lives in central California with her husband, dogs, and horse. Right now she is working on a chapbook called "Love Psychosis"—poems about the madness of love.

JOANNE GRAM is a queer poet in Lansing, Michigan. She has an MPA from Western Michigan University. Her poetry appears in publications, including *Of Rust and Glass* issues, issues of the *East Lansing Art Festival Poetry Journal*, *Writing in a Woman's Voice*, the *Lansing Secret Treasure Collection*, and multiple Peninsula Poets collections. Joanne hopes you read her work and perhaps hear her read at the many open mics in Lansing.

STEPHANIE RENÉE PAYNE (she/her/hers) earned her MFA from Vermont College of Fine Arts. She lives and writes in her native Los Angeles. Her writing has appeared in *Hunger Mountain*, the *Los Angeles Review*, *For Harriet*, *Gemini Magazine*, and elsewhere. Payne is currently an associate professor in the writing program at the University of Southern California and also teaches for Mindful USC.

HAMPTON WILLIAMS HOFER lives in Raleigh, North Carolina, where she writes and raises babies. Her work has appeared in *Flying South*, *WALTER* magazine, *Architectural Digest*, and *Food 52*, among others. She has degrees from the University of Virginia and New York University's Writers Workshop in Paris.

LAURA E. GARRARD, a 2022 Tieton LiTFUSE poetry scholar, holds a master's in journalism from UT-Knoxville. She was an editor and proofreader for Country Music Foundation Press, Thomas Nelson, and Rutledge Hill Press, and contributed to the *Journal of Country Music*. She is the recipient of four scholarships from Centrum Writers Conference. Her poetry has appeared in *The Madrona Project*, *Tidepools*, *Poets of the Promise*, *Teton Spirit*, and others. A cancer thriver, she writes from her home in Olympic National Park and supports clients' healing through bodywork in Port Angeles, Washington.

ROBIN PERCYZ (she/her) is a queer writer living in the New York metropolitan region, spending the majority of her career as a content manager. She has overseen content staff at online marketing and website design firms, designed weekly newsletters for a Modern Orthodox High School, and has served as a member of the Society for Menstrual Cycle Research. She was invited to present her piece "Boxing and Bleeding" at their conference "Re: Cycling" in 2011 where Gloria Steinem was in attendance. Robin was a competitive amateur boxer for four years, fighting twice in the New York Daily News Golden Gloves competition. She has recently discovered her love for writing poetry, after years of admiring it as a reader. If she can help others feel visible through her work, she will consider that success.

CONNIE CORZILIUS grew up in Granite City, Illinois, and currently lives in Augusta, Georgia. Her work is forthcoming or has appeared in *Bodega*

Magazine, JewishFiction.net, Another Chicago Magazine, Calyx, Mississippi Review, Big Muddy, Stonecoast Review, and elsewhere. She was awarded the Women's National Book Association Short Fiction Award, and she's been nominated for a Pushcart Prize and the Million Writers Award. A graduate of the Iowa Writers' Workshop, she was a bookseller and a writer/editor for the bookselling and publishing trade for many years.

STEPHANIE WHETSTONE earned her BA from Duke University and her MFA in creative writing from UNC-Greensboro. She has been a fellow at VCCA and Hambidge, and a Peter Taylor Scholar at the Sewanee Writers' Conference. Her fiction has appeared in *Waccamaw, Waypoints, Drafthorse,* the *Anthology of Appalachian Writers,* and *Narrative.* Her novel, *Deep Belly of the Earth,* was a finalist for the Lee Smith Novel Prize, and her essay, "Mathitudes," received the North Carolina Writers' Network Rose Post award. She is the assistant director of Princeton Writes and lives in Brooklyn.

SUSAN JENSEN is a happy spirit on a creative rampage! After (too) many years teaching high school English, speech, journalism, drama, debate, and creative writing, and eighteen years in show business, she was able to retire to a Whidbey Island paradise off the coast of Seattle, open up an Airbnb, and become an award-winning writer and artist. Life is good. Finally. The rest is fodder for writing projects. Careful—you may end up in one of them . . . Go visit her Airbnb (airbnb.com/slink/YYJTEOSN)!

ERIN ROBERTSON teaches outdoor nature writing classes in Boulder County, Colorado (@bocowildwriters). Her poetry has been published in the *North American Review, Cold Mountain Review, Poet Lore, Deep Wild,* and elsewhere, and has been performed by Ars Nova Singers and The Crossing choir. Past honors include being a guest artist hosted by the US Consulate in Kazakhstan, Voices of the Wilderness Artist in Residence at Koyukuk National Wildlife Refuge in Alaska, Boulder County Artist in Residence at Caribou Ranch, and awards in the Michael

Adams Poetry Prize and Columbine Poets Members' Contest. She lives in Louisville, Colorado, with her remarkable husband, two sons, parakeet, and pup, who teach her about wonder every day.

ELINOR DAVIS was born in Iowa and led a peripatetic early life, eventually settling in Northern California. After graduating university with a sociology major and realizing she had no marketable skills, she also got a nursing degree and license, just in case writing short stories didn't pay the bills. She lives with her daughter and grandchildren on an urban homestead, where she helps weed the garden and works as a writer/editor specializing in health care topics. Her fiction and nonfiction have appeared in numerous US and international publications. "The Cambium Layer" is part of a collection-in-progress of linked stories about several generations of a large Midwestern family.

Made in United States
Troutdale, OR
05/26/2024

20146268R00077